RUPAMATI

RUPAMATI

by
Rudra Raj Pandey

Translated from the Nepali by
Shanti Mishra

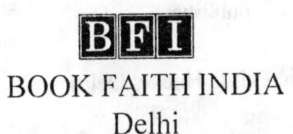
BOOK FAITH INDIA
Delhi

RUPAMATI

Published by
BOOK FAITH INDIA
414-416 Express Tower,
Azadpur Commercial Complex
Delhi, India 110 033

Distributed by
PILGRIMS BOOK HOUSE
P.O Box 3872, Kathmandu, Nepal
P.O Box 38, Varanasi, India
Tel: 977-1-424942
Fax: 977-1-424943
E-mail: info@pilgrims.wlink.com.np

Cover Photo: A scene from the Nepal Television serial "RUPAMATI"
Layout by Hom K.C.

ISBN 81-7303-102-9

1st English Edition
Copyright © 1999 Shanti Mishra
All rights reserved

The contents of this book may not be reproduced, stored or copied in any form – printed, electronic, photocopied or otherwise – except for excerpts used in reviews, without the written permission of the publisher.

Produced by Graphic Prints House, Delhi.

Printed at : Jay Kay Offset Printers
Shed No. 17, DSIDC (SFS) Cat. II, Rohtak Road, Nangloi, Delhi-41

About the Author

Rudra Raj Pandey was born in 1901 in Kathmandu, into a family whose ancestors had been preceptors of the Gorkha Shah dynasty. He was drawn to an academic career, and studied history up to the master's level in Allahabad. In 1924, he accepted a professorship at Trichandra College and the headmastership of Darbar High School, both in Kathmandu. During his tenure he succeeded in getting the tenth-class School Leaving Certificate examination shifted from India to Nepal to provide study opportunities for members of lower castes. Following the end of Rana rule in 1950, he became the director of the Department of Archaeology. Later, in 1954, he was appointed chairman of the Nepal National Education Commission, set up to devise a comprehensive educational system for Nepal. In 1965 he took over the vice-chancellorship of Tribhuvan University where, during his period in office, he was instrumental in establishing the Centre for Nepal and Asian Studies and in initiating postgraduate courses for Sanskrit and science. His literary interests took shape early on. He played a key role in getting native works published and foreign works translated, and in establishing the influential literary journal *Sharada*. Rudra Raj Pandey wrote essays, plays, histories of both India and England, and five novels, of which *Rupamati* was his first, and has remained his best loved. He died in 1990.

About the Translator

Shanti Mishra's life, like that of Rudra Raj Pandey, has centred on education and service to the nation, and in literary pursuits as well. The first girl in her Newar community to complete ten years of schooling, she went on, again like Rudra Raj Pandey, to study history in India. She returned to later serve under him, among others, at Tribhuvan University as the first chief librarian of the Central Library. She is the founding president of the Nepal branch of P.E.N. International. Her book, *Voice of Truth*, a stirring personal account of eventful years in Nepal's history, has been a highly acclaimed number one bestseller since its publication in 1994.

Translator's Dedication
For the novelists of Nepal

Preface to the English Translation

Nineteen thirty-four was the year that started off with an earthquake shaking the Kathmandu Valley and reducing much of it to rubble. The Rana prime minister at the time, Juddha Samsher, was in the far west of the country hunting, and it took some days for the news to reach him, and several more weeks for him to return to the capital. Once there, though, he proved adept at organizing the recovery effort and getting things moving again.

Rudra Raj Pandey, then in his ninth year as the first Nepalese principal of Nepal's first secondary school, Darbar High School in Kathmandu, himself organized a brigade of volunteers to aid the earthquake victims, for which he later would receive a decoration from King Tribhuvan—one of many such acts of recognition for a life devoted to service to the nation. He would come to be called Sardar (a particular civil service rank, but with the more general meaning of leader) as a mark of respect.

Within six months of the disaster, Rudra Raj Pandey did something that was earthshaking in its own way: he published what is now generally considered to be the first modern novel in Nepali, *Rupamati*. Novels, to be sure, had already been written in the language, but they lay little claim to being something uniquely Nepalese. One may characterize these early attempts as falling into one of two categories, conveniently distinguished according to the two chief aims of literature recognized by classical authors, namely instruction or delight.[1] Thus the first group, offering instruction, comprised works that retold tales from the Puranas and other devotional literature; the second

---

[1] These two aims correlate with religious experience, and follow one from the other, as may be illustrated in a number of psalms from the Bible. Thus the last verse of Psalm 16—"Thou wilt show me the path of life: in thy presence is fullness of joy: at thy right hand there are pleasures for evermore"—could well be taken as what a reader seeks from serious literature. Instruction in this sense, of course, goes beyond mere moral guidance to a revelatory vision of life; and delight, beyond titillation.

category, a whole range of what may be called adventure novels out of the past and foreign climes.

What Rudra Raj Pandey did was to write a story that any reader could recognize as true to the country and the times, and at once both instructive and delightful. Its subject was *buhartan*, the duties of a daughter-in-law, which in modern times had come to be enforced, by mothers-in-law in particular, with undue strictness. The novel was instantly popular, and has remained so ever since. Shanti Mishra has long felt the need to see this seminal work translated into English, and the fruits of her labour will now thankfully make it available to a broader range of readers.

The fictional account is to a certain extent autobiographical. Rudra Raj Pandey, like the husband of Rupamati, the novel's main character, was redirected by a mentor away from a Sanskrit- to an English-based education, and received a scholarship from the government to pursue higher studies in India where, again like Mr. Sharma, he came into closer contact with Western culture, only to moderate his enthusiasm for it later. In fact, he ended up a devoted Hindu, took initiation, attained powers and came to be regarded in India, where he spent much time, as a saint.

In an account of one of his spiritual preceptors, Gopal Baba, the author has this to say about the role of women:

> ... the seers ... considered the ideal wife to be one who was ever inspiring her husband towards the godly path. The husband had to fight the battles of life. It was the wife who held the household together. [...] The wife's sole duty was to live a pure life, prepare nourishing food, walk the way of the Lord and devote herself to the service of her husband.

Insofar as *buhartan* had assumed extreme forms, the author saw it as standing in the way of this traditional ideal. Bhanubhakta Acharya, the father of Nepali literature, had written a versified tract on the duties of a daughter-in-law in the middle of the nineteenth century, at a time when they were still regarded as part of a broad spiritual *paideia*, not as admission rites. The modern aberration lent itself to modern imaginative treatment, and Rudra Raj Pandey boldly seized on the form of a novel, while at the same time remaining true to his traditional outlook.

Two possible reactions to the custom of strict *buhartan* are considered: extreme submission and extreme revolt—and both occurring within the same family. Rupamati takes the first path and goes through a series of trials up to the eleventh chapter, the very middle of the book,[2] when a holy man pronounces the blessing of a grandson upon her father within the sacred precincts of Pashupatinath. Meanwhile the second daughter-in-law, Baral's daughter, who is introduced in Chapter 5, has turned the tables on her mother-in-law, treating her as her inferior, and her fellow daughter-in-law as beneath contempt.

The total conception is like a Shakespearean comedy, and indeed much of the book is constructed in the form of straight dialogue. There are a wealth of minor characters, some of whose names produce a comic effect on readers of Nepali similar to that of the Bard's on the English-speaking world. There is a confused medley of near kin with more or less poor opinions of one another. We learn, for instance, from a gathering at a female relative of Rupamati's father-in-law, Pandit Chavilal, that the latter had spent much of his life cheating people out of their rightfully earned money. His nickname, it emerges, was Chwanke, used for a

---

[2]Chapter 17, whose exaggerated length in the original is perhaps meant to replicate the seeming interminableness of the consequences of moral fall, has in the translation been divided into two chapters. While perhaps unfair to the author's intent, this does make all chapters of fairly equal duration and, incidentally, the critical eleventh chapter now literally the middle one of the book.

man with irregular teeth. Of Baral's daughter, too, we are elsewhere told that she has an uncomely set of her own, she being the one who filches food from her mother-in-law and jewels from her parents. The effect is to dissolve the dichotomy between the city- and country-born, the educated and the illiterate: their characters are the same. The Nepal family into which Rupamati has married (it is a typical surname) stands quite evidently for the nation as a whole, with the author's ideal being expressed in the main character's married name, which translates as "Beautiful Nepal."

Some six years after the earthquake and the publication of *Rupamati*, Juddha Samsher would start rounding up writers who were suspected of casting masked aspersions on the Rana regime. Inquisitions were held, and works were picked apart for any seditious allusions. Rudra Raj Pandey was too stellar a personality to invite suspicion, but if the rulers had read his work carefully they would perhaps have seen that they, too, were fair targets of the author's criticism. Of the two son's, Mr. Sharma was spellbound by English culture, and Ravilal pursued a riotous form of life—two of the Ranas' own main traits. And was not *buhartan* itself, as practised at the time, a fitting metaphor for Rana rule? The Ranas, however, lacked a Rupamati to work her subtle change upon them, and they were eventually swept from power. What the times called for was a return to the true values of the past and a judicious acceptance of what the new age had to offer. It is this middle path that the novel extols, and that the life of its author exemplifies.

Philip H. Pierce
Kathmandu

Chapter 1

"Hey, Chameli! Oh, Chameli, Chameli! Is that daughter-in-law of ours still sleeping? Hasn't that daughter-in-law of ours woken up? She must be still all sprawled out. The sun's rays have already reached Babulal's roof. Disgusting! Modern girls have no shame. Go and tell her a crow will come and prick her." The sound of such grumbling entered Rupamati's ears during that enjoyable time when sleep had left her but drowsiness was telling her, Wait a moment, wait a moment.

Her morning saw her get up before sunrise, sweep the house from top to bottom, smear the entrance with a mixture of cow dung and red clay, clean all pots and pans, prepare for worship and sort out the vegetables. If towards midday, after the first meal, she managed to lull her mother-in-law to sleep by massaging her legs, she might win one or two hours of free time. Then she would at least be spared the nagging, even if she still had to twist wicks into shape. The rest of the time there was a steady stream of nit-picking. She plunged into a day of do this and do that. Come evening, darkness set in as she was performing worship or twisting more wicks.

Her father-in-law, who was the priest of the colonel of Battisputali, never came home before nine. Everyone in the family called for their rice and then fell into the lap of the goddess of sleep. But Rupamati had to help Chameli do the dishes. Her mother-in-law had allowed the latter to take things into her head, and the result was that she didn't care a fig for anyone else's opinion. This was how the days passed.

The previous day had been the Teej[1] day of fasting. What was poor Rupamati to do? While the thirteen-year-

---

[1] A day in August-September when women fast, bathe and pray for the long life of their husbands.

old was telling herself to get up, the shouting of a flower seller—"*Svam mala*"[2]—awakened her mother-in-law.

Rupamati sprang out of bed and began sweeping up the refuse. Her mother-in-law's mouth did not cease to give forth, but since her grumbling was a daily occurrence, it had come to seem as ordinary as a dish of rice and grams. In the meantime Pandit Chavilal woke up. Chameli filled the hookah with tobacco and brought it to him—a must as soon as he arose. He set the hookah gurgling, and then his wife entered the room, spouting off about how the late rise of their daughter-in-law by half an hour was an unpardonable crime. She began telling the whole story to her husband. "How shameless the women of this Kali-yuga[3] are! I've been shouting since the cock crowed, and she still doesn't get up! If we had behaved that way, what would our mothers-in-law have done to us? Working day and night didn't satisfy them."

The pandit had no interest in her story at all, having his own worries to ponder. He was much given to thinking things over while smoking. This was his time to commune with himself. His failure to utter a sound plunged his wife into despair. Her shouting became even louder.

"It's because her father-in-law is spoiling her, isn't it? Would she be off in a world of her own for no reason at all? Chameli. Hey, Chameli, come, come! Let Rupamati do what she likes. It's out of my hands." She went babbling out of the room.

Pandit Chavilal broke out into a profuse sweat. At every little irritation his wife let out her anger; what trifle was behind today's outburst? He thought it over a bit and arrived at the conclusion that the main reason for her rise in temper had been the fasting the previous night to celebrate Teej. Just then his young son Ravilal woke up and began crying, "Mother, Mother!" A hero emerged to

---

[2] A Newari expression meaning "Do you need flowers?"

[3] The fourth of four ages of the world, and the one in which we are now living—a period of calamities and disasters when virtue has ceased to hold sway.

save the pandit from the plague that that day brought. Hearing her son's call, Chavilal's wife stopped her descent one floor down and returned. As it was, she was slightly hesitant to storm out of the house so, for fear of what her neighbours might say.

The pandit seized his chance and bellowed out an abuse at his daughter-in-law. His wife's feelings were assuaged. She had gained a victory. Now who would be unmoved by her lion roar? The innocent daughter-in-law had no recourse but to grind her teeth and suppress the anger that arose from the gratuitous reproof. The Mahabharata war had come to an end after eighteen days. There was a Mahabharata war now going on in Pandit Chavilal's house, but nobody knew how long it would last.

Every day something came between mother-in-law and daughter-in-law. Everyone was amazed by the latter's powers of endurance. It would have been difficult to admit that she knew no faults at her age, but the mistakes she committed were minor. The pandit's wife, though, didn't even consider that they might be of human origin. It was her custom to make a buffalo out of a flea, a mountain out of a molehill. She had no feel for appearances—the need to keep domestic affairs domestic. Her instinct was to sound the drum. The senior women among her neighbours would come, and hours passed in discussion. When the topic of daughters-in-law came up, they began reciting their lore. All the other women criticized their own daughters-in-law. Madam Pandit, however, was in a league of her own. Everyone truckled to her; everyone came out with a "Well, I declare!" for the old lady. It is the nature of humans to join in the uproar, and she was pleasantly surprised.

Another gathering of mothers-in-law took place three or four days later. Madam Pandit took the chair. The main subject of discussion was "Modern Daughters-in-law—Useless, Naughty, Coquettish." Narahari's aunt from next door got things rolling by telling what had happened to her. "Just consider the outrage! During the Teej festival I had to fast and keep the oil lamp burning the whole night. I felt so sleepy I dozed right off. 'Take care of things,' I told my daughter-in-law. The next day, when we returned from bathing in the Bagmati, she went to bed claiming to have a fever. No consideration at all for my having fasted! That she should pick that of all days to have a fever, the sinful creature! The doctor hasn't allowed her to eat anything these past three or four days—a fitting punishment for having staged her little show!" Other ladies chimed in. Narahari's aunt was delighted. No sympathy was expressed for the daughter-in-law "on her deathbed."

Now it was the turn of the captain's wife. Her anger over her daughter-in-law was even greater. She said, "All of you tell me if it wasn't utterly shameless of her to say, just a day before Teej, that she was having her period. Would our mothers-in-law have tolerated it if we had done something like that? I had to do everything the day of fasting: prepare the articles of worship, soak the wicks, visit Pashupati,[4] perform the worship and tend the oil lamp—utterly exhausting!" Each added her "Hear! Hear!" to the next. The captain's wife was pleased.

Rame's mother came forward and said, "None of you can ever have seen such a despicable daughter-in-law as my Rame's wife. My husband brought four *barphi*s, eight *jilebi*s, ten *svari*s[5] and four mangoes from Rani Saheb for me to enjoy on the day before Teej. I set aside two of everything to eat at bedtime, thinking I'd be hungry the next day, and distributed all the rest to the children. Then I go and what do I see but just one left, the other gone. I knew she'd be ravenous, so I'd already treated her to some *roti*s[6] and molasses. I gave her braid a few nice tugs before I finished with her." There was a peel of laughter at this declamation. All approved of her form of chastisement.

The colonel's wife came forward. "If you all had to put up with how my daughter-in-law performs her duties, I

---

[4]Nepal's national shrine on the outskirts of Kathmandu, dedicated to Lord Shiva.

[5]Typical Nepalese sweets.

[6]Flat, circular unleavened bread, prepared from wheat and heated over a flame.

don't know what you'd do. On the day before Teej she started in to clarify some butter for the *sel*.[7] When she transferred it to the pot, she spilled about a pint of it. I go take a look and find she's burnt her hands and whatnot, and the ghee all over the floor. I couldn't control myself. I grabbed her and said, 'You witch, what wealth did you bring from your father? Come on now, out with your purse!' I didn't let the little lynx eat a thing that day."

"Bravo! Well done!"—thus the warm reception accorded by the circle of mothers-in-law.

The chairwoman's turn had come. She, too, gave a spicy description of her own daughter-in-law's "deeds of valour." Many supported the notion that the punishment given to daughters-in-law was not what it should be. The resolution that modern-day daughters-in-law were good for nothing passed unanimously.

Rupamati was all ears during this discussion. She uttered a prayer to herself: "O Lord, why did you send me to this world to become a daughter-in-law? If the fate written on my forehead[8] had been to become a mother-in-law, I would not have to perform all these chores today." Few in number are those in this world who can be a mother-in-law without first being a daughter-in-law. Such lucky ones would have to come within the coils of a widower—another state of distress! Moreover, they would not be accorded many days of control over their step-daughters-in-law. Thus the strange rule was ordained by the Creator that without participating in household affairs as a daughter-in-law, no woman would ever become a mother-in-law.

☙❧

---

[7] A donut-like pastry.

[8] The god Chitragupta is said to write a child's destiny on its forehead on the sixth day after birth. Oil lamps are ritually burned, and a bracelet is given to the baby.

Chapter 2

Pandit Chavilal was a high-caste Brahmin. His ancestors had obtained some land from a pleasure-loving soul for the great entertainment they had afforded him by staging a partridge fight. The pandit was accordingly proud of his property. His ancestral home was in Panchamane. Villagers from his hometown came once or twice a year to pay him a visit. He couldn't help but show off to them in a big way; he put on a display of luxury and proved to them that he was somebody, smoking a cigarette clamped between his lips. If he normally had to go out at eleven, he left at nine, and returned just before the cannon[9] signalled everyone to be home. His visitors from the hills were struck with wonder.

One day a nephew of his uncle came. Being educated, he found jobs reciting religious texts during the Dasain festival.[10] That uncle was the one who had sent the fifty or a hundred rupees in annual revenues from Panchamane, so they couldn't refuse to put up his nephew. They were afraid, though, that if he stayed with them for a longer period, he would spread abroad how things really were in the household. In spite of Madam Pandit's strong opposition, she could do nothing. They had to let him stay. Her husband tried his best to explain the situation to her in bed at night. "Look, don't let things get out of hand. It wasn't easy to impress upon the villagers how well-to-do we are, but I did it. Don't you notice how they gather around us whenever we go there? Be on your guard. And keep our daughter-in-law on hers." As the pandit continued to lecture away, his wife started snoring.

---

[9]A practice introduced by Dev Shamsher in 1901 to ensure that everyone was in by ten o'clock.
[10]The major Hindu festival celebrated in September-October in honour of the goddess Durga.

The first two days of the festival passed without incident. The third day, however, concern arose that they might have to feed their nonpaying guest with no end in sight. Revati had come back, his recitation duties now over. There was still some daily worship left for him to perform, so he went straight into the prayer-room, but no sooner had he done so than he heard the sound of Madam Pandit's whispering. A conversation was in progress between her and her neighbour's old wet-nurse.

"How unlucky I am! I've got troubles enough with my own family—and then these useless guests to put up with. There are too many of them in our house. We're never to ourselves. My husband had his meal long ago. How long do I have to wait for this other fellow?"

Upon hearing this complaint, Revati went to the dining room without bothering to recite his prayers. On that day he didn't know whether he was chewing dirt or chewing rice.

Ravilal was always making trouble for his sister-in-law. Whenever she made wicks for oil lamps, he would tear them to pieces. Whenever she performed rituals he spit at her. That same day Rupamati was dipping the wicks in oil when her brother-in-law came and upset the oil she had placed on the churn. Rupamati feared her mother-in-law would beat her. "What have you gone and done, for goodness' sake? Now what's there to dip the wicks in?"

As soon as she uttered these few words, Ravilal began whining and hollering. Rupamati's mother-in-law was resting in her bedroom at the time. Hearing her son, she set off in his direction, with repeated gaspings of "Why are you crying?"

Ravilal knew his mother's temperament, and from the daily routine understood her relationship with his sister-in-law. As soon as he heard his mother's voice, he began to cry and scream even louder. His mother reached the spot only to find oil all over the floor, her son rolling about wantonly and her daughter-in-law busy counting wicks. Hardly had she repeated her question when Ravilal let out with new sobs, saying, "She was the one who spilt the oil, and then she whacked me."

That was enough for the pandit's wife. She began to roar, "Who do you think you're raising your hand against, you witch? Has your father ever given him one paisa that you have the right to beat him? Neither my husband nor I ever lay a hand on him. Such a shoddy piece of footwear yourself and yet so proud?"

The daughter-in-law's face turned red, the mother-in-law's reproach being intolerable in her state of innocence. "I did nothing to Ravilal." This was said with diffidence, in a soft voice with words that barely came out.

That set her up for the attack of a tigress. "Now see here, you shameless vixen! You're saying that Ravilal tells lies? What could he gain by lying? If you didn't beat him, would he be sobbing all this time? You let your hand go to work on him and then come up with a tall tale. What deceit! I'll bet anything you knocked the oil over when you stretched out your hand to strike. You hussy, you haven't brought enough property from your father to be wasting things in this way. I won't allow the money my husband earns by sweating blood to go down the drain like this." All these words she managed to get out with one breath, while at the same time pulling poor Rupamati's braid and lips. By this time the whole household had gathered to see the show. No one dared to speak. All the windows that looked out onto the neighbouring courtyard opened up.

Such virulent excesses were daily fare, but something strange had happened on that day. The energy that erupted after having been held three or four days in check was like the rush of water from a burst dam a fisherman had set to catch fish in. No one had the strength to control it. Revati at first looked on agape. When he saw his sister-in-law being cruelly tormented, a two-way battle arose within him between pity and fear. In the end he couldn't summon up his courage. And how could he? When the fire of anger blazes up in a woman's heart, she loses her senses. Even as nobody dares warm himself at a wildfire, so too wrath's flames burn with an unbearable heat. Moreover, all mothers-in-law turn into lionesses in the presence of their daughters-in-law. Who would have it in him to approach such a beast? That's why Revati couldn't summon up his courage.

During that day's altercation Madam Pandit had had no sense that the clock was ticking. At last she was left with a sweet taste in her mouth; now the circle of mothers-in-law couldn't say she had administered too little punishment. She wouldn't have to listen to words that made her heart stand still. "I scratched her face and snatched her braid. About half a litre of oil must have spilled; I charged her for one. I really showed my stuff!"

Madam Pandit was absorbed in her thoughts. Rice and grams were not fetched from the store on time. Pandit Chavilal came back tired and sighing after a whole day's work. Revati had spread out, and was reading, the *Gorkhapatra*.[11] He didn't notice the pandit's arrival. The nephew was downcast, like a chicken that has taken salt. Why had he come to stay in this house? They had such a reputation and name in the village! What would the villagers say if they knew the real situation there? Such thoughts flooded in on his mind, though his eyes were on the paper.

Seeing him, the pandit thought the state his house was in not good; the cat must have got out of the bag. He fell to worrying. "Why so blue, my boy? Have you had your meal?"

These questions were posed, and Revati reacted with a start; then only had he noticed the pandit's presence. "No, I suppose it's not ready yet," he replied. He said nothing else.

The rice was still not cooked—a state of affairs that was beginning to turn the pandit's stomach into a playground. He went upstairs wondering what obstacles his wife might have created and why the Brahmin cook was behind schedule. He looked and saw the rice just coming to a boil, his wife beginning to recite some religious verses on a twelve-cubit-long mat, and Chameli preparing the tobacco. He did not speak, went back downstairs and began to smoke. Finally the words "Dinner's ready!" echoed in the room.

---

[11] The government Nepali daily.

After dinner the pandit never felt sleepy unless he smoked his hookah. His wife arrived after he had lain down on the bed. Her grumbling began. She scaled down her own faults and spiced up her daughter-in-law's; she appeared in a good light and put her daughter-in-law in a bad one. The day's court session came to an end.

The pandit was seized with anger, yet he offered no argument, thinking it better to listen on in silence. What had happened was done and over; why make the night a torment?

The next day the performer of rituals went out to perform but did not return. They waited with the meal one hour. There was no sign of him. The pandit heard the whole story when he returned in the evening.

☼☋

Chapter 3

Rupamati began to long for the day when she could go back to her parents' home to receive the annual *tika*,[12] the agony was unbearable. The Dasain festival! When it came she would eat, drink and wear patterned clothing; nowadays alpaca saris in dazzling patterns were available during this period of fashionableness and self-gratification. Rupamati had to torture her back and shed bitter tears. She had long ago convinced herself, on the basis of the rain of abuse, that it was in the nature of the garrulous old woman to grumble. She herself would not neglect her own work. Let her go on shouting. She would not demean herself. This Dasain, though, her mother-in-law had slapped her for no reason, so that things had become intolerable. She began to think of her parents' home.

Rupamati was married at an early age. Her father was a pandit from a respectable family—strongly conservative and traditional. He spent two to three hours in the morning just worshipping and praying. It was a rule for him not to eat unless he had completed a thousand recitations of the Gayatri.[13] It was said that he used to delight the god Bhairavnath by conversing with him. His whole family line had been tantrics with unusual powers. The last of them, Pandit Mohan Prasad Luintel, may not have had any asafoetida but he did have a pouch for it; which is as much as to say that he may not have had tantric powers but he did have a reputation for having them.

The current pandit's neighbours and friends rushed to him for advice whenever some problem arose. In

---

[12] A mark of vermilion or similar pigment placed on the forehead as a blessing.
[13] The most famous verse of the Veda, a prayer directed to the sun. A thousand recitations of it daily ensures a person of heaven.

addition, the pandit had a certain command of astrology. Some came to ask for an auspicious time to pierce the ear of their children, some to ask how many days they should mourn the death of the daughter of their father's sister, and some troubled him by asking what kind of donation was dignified for giving to priests on the day of Baman Dvadasi.[14] In this manner the pandit passed his life, giving advice to all who came to him for consultation. Nor did he have trouble providing for himself. He had first-class rice fields in Manohara—handed down from his great-grandfather—which yielded four hundred maunds of paddy. It was low-lying land, and never affected by drought. Income from the Terai[15] amounted to from two to four hundred rupees annually.

The pandit had a small family. His sole claim to wealth in offspring was his daughter Rupamati, whom he gave in marriage at the age of seventy-two months, as required by religious texts. His wife was also upright, pious and understanding; she walked in the way of her husband, not transgressing his commands—a rare nature indeed. It must be said that the pandit was very lucky to have found such an ideal jewel of a woman in this Kali-yuga.

Luintelni Bajyai[16] was up before the cock had time to crow. She bathed and so forth, and then put all the worship utensils her husband would need for the daily rites in the prayer-room so that everything would be in its proper place when he looked for it. The morning meal was ready even before her husband could finish his worship. The servants were also well disciplined, trained to obey all orders so that no problems arose. The kitchen for its part was always spick and span, and encircled with saucers and dishes full of tasty things.

Eating the food served by his ever-smiling wife, the pandit felt contentment. He spent daylight hours paging through religious books. In the evening he sometimes

---

[14] A day in August-September commemorating Vishnu's avatar as a dwarf who overcame the evil designs of King Bali.

[15] The plains in the southern part of Nepal.

[16] "Bajyai" is a title of respect applied to older women or to any Brahmin woman. When used with a family name, the latter takes the feminine ending -*ni*.

managed to visit Pashupati temple and would come back after seeing the offering of oil and ghee lamps; at other times he remembered Vasuki's chastity[17] and considered himself blessed; and at still other times he made it all the way to Pachali temple to chant the name of Ram. Usually, though, he performed his chanting at the Bagmati River, and having done so returned home. He passed his days in a life of ease.

But even this family, though immersed in a sea of happiness, was from time to time plagued with great worries. When Rupamati began describing, with eyes full of tears, the needless treatment she had had to put up with from her mother-in-law, even a stone heart would have melted, so how could her mother's heart not be rent? But her mother was very astute; she did not want to spoil her daughter with vain indulgences of "Oh, you poor thing!" Yes, she certainly felt unbearable anguish, but she didn't want to admit it and encourage defiance in her beloved daughter by supporting everything she said. After all, her daughter could not spend the whole of her life in her parents' home. There was no other alternative but to go back to her husband's. Her mother consoled her by comparing the story of her agony with other similar stories so that Rupamati would have the full power to endure her torment. The people in the neighbourhood were amazed to see how zealously Luintelni Bajyai went about setting her daughter on the right path. She could do so only because she had a big heart.

Rupamati had come into this world to bring light to the dim, sonless family of Pandit Mohan Prasad. Wishing a son, Luintelni Bajyai had promised to offer one hundred thousand oil lamps to the god Santaneshvar[18] were her wish to come true. It would have been difficult to say how many had reassured her, on the basis of her good qualities, with the words, "You're sure to get a son. Don't worry!"

---

[17] A temple in the courtyard of the Pashupatinath complex is dedicated to the snake god Vasuki.

[18] The god who has power to bless his devotees with children.

The ways of the world are strange. How boldly people assert that something will happen, failing to consider what fate may hold in store. As if to prove everyone's reasoning wrong, Rupamati was born. When they learned of the outcome many people's countenances fell. They set about putting the best face on things. "It's okay to have a daughter first; your next child has to be son." But Luintelni Bajyai's unhappiness didn't last long. She was joyed to see such bright features, a form in which the Lord's workmanship so fully shone forth. She began bringing up her daughter on hugs and squeezes. The daughter grew apace, like the waxing moon. At five years of age she was taught a bit of reading. Wishing to give his daughter in marriage when she reached seventy-two months, the pandit began to look around for a bridegroom. Since he had no other offspring, arranging a marriage at such an early age meant not a little sorrow, but he was a man of the old school, and didn't know how to cater to the times. His persistence was correspondingly great.

Pandit Virupakshya was the house priest. He brought news about prospective grooms. As there were no other sons or daughters, and as the family had fairly large holdings of tax-free rice fields, the people came in droves. "I don't want a rich groom; it's enough if he's a boy of merit and has begun studies," the house priest was told.

After a long search a boy of nine who was studying the *Laghukaumudi*[19] was found. The boy was uncommonly intelligent. Young though he was, he could explain the meaning of small poetical texts, and provide grammatical and etymological commentary at the same time. He was, in addition, of good ancestry. The family of Nepalese from Panchamane were not of low status. The Lord provided abundantly for their needs both day and night. And the boy's appearance was not something that invited negative comment. It was decided to give Rupamati to him. The marriage took place with great

---

[19] A famous Sanskrit grammar.

fanfare on the day of Sri Panchami[20] in the month of Magh. The pandit thought that, now that he had succeeded in giving his daughter away at seventy-two months, no one had it in their power to close the doors of heaven on him.

Poor Rupamati was forced to become the slave of others from the age of seven. She didn't have the slightest idea what sort of strange bird a groom might be and how she should behave with him. Nobody cared at all about this since she was a child bride coming from a rich family. Invitees found inspecting the dowry on the wedding day unendurable for the envy it caused, and some relations began sedulously to find fault with Rupamati. A number argued persuasively that, even though the girl was of unsurpassed beauty, her lips were dried and sored, others that her eyebrows were small, and still others that her ear had a mole on it. Rupamati returned to her parents' house after completing sixteen days of ritual, so nobody could make any comments.

Rupamati's mother-in-law was so happy that she could hardly keep her feet on the ground. Her son received a gold coin as an offering from his in-laws. And the old woman herself received the standard *tilahari*[21] during a visit to the bride's family. The Teej feast of that year was really a feast—full of sweets, *sels*, *puris*[22] and *achar*.[23] That year, therefore, passed in unmitigated joy.

Rupamati, so young a girl, began to receive training at her parents' home. Luintelni Bajyai did her utmost to make her daughter as well endowed as she herself was with all good qualities. She had her regularly study Bhanubhakta's version of the *Ramayana*.[24] Arithmetic was

---

[20] A festival in January-February to honour Sarasvati, the goddess of learning.

[21] A necklace of beads on which a cylinder of gold is strung, usually given by the groom to the bride on their wedding day.

[22] A type of deep-fried bread made of wheat flour.

[23] A hot, sour, cooked or seasoned vegetable dish taken in small amounts with rice and grams.

[24] The classic 18th-century rendition of the Indian epic by the father of Nepali literature.

mastered up to multiplication and division. She taught her to make leaf-plates and wicks for oil lamps, and to cook various delicacies. She also gave her some idea of how to be a good daughter-in-law. In this way, Rupamati's bearing was being refined. She had come to have a good grasp of things. This was the reason she was able to put up with her mother-in-law's excesses.

After three or four years Rupamati began to menstruate. She could no longer stay at her parents' place but had to live with her in-laws. Some months passed happily. She was given ten or twelve rupees by her parents to buy a morsel when she become hungry. One day she was so famished that she sent a servant to purchase some *gulabjamuns*[25] for a quarter of a rupee. From the time her mother-in-law had heard of that, she had been envious—just to be envious. Moreover, the daughter-in-law's childlike and impetuous nature, and the fact that she occasionally wore frocks she had brought along with her from home, was likewise destined to raise her mother-in-law's hackles. The spark that came out of all this produced combustion within, and then became a huge blaze that Rupamati could hardly tolerate. Thus she looked forward to the *tika* festival with great longing.

ಲ‍ೞ

---

[25] A round brown sweet made from thickened milk and dipped in syrup.

Chapter 4

Mr. H. L. Sharma[26] was the eldest son of Pandit Chavilal. By the age of ten he had already completed study of the *Laghukaumudi* and displayed an uncommon acquaintance with word analysis. All the teachers of Durbar Sanskrit School were pleased with him. Whenever they met Chavilal they praised his son, and the pandit beamed. No one in the school obtained such good marks as he had in the first-level examination. The pandits were certain he would stand first in the mid-level examination in Benares. Luintel Baje[27] had given away his daughter after hearing all this.

The colonel and his cronies used to study English. Their tutor, Pyaremohan Saksena, took favourable notice of the boy. Seeing his intelligence, he formed the idea of teaching him English too. Since the boy's father was an old-time visitor to his doorstep, and the colonel's dear friend to boot, the tutor raised the question. The pandit was somewhat reluctant, but when he heard the opinion he kept quiet and did not refuse.

News of the son-in-law's learning English reached the father-in-law. The latter began to sweat profusely; his lips and palate turned dry. What act of impiety was in the works? Had he given his daughter to him so that he could do that? It was written in the Hindu code of law: *Na pathet yaminibhasham na gachhet jainamandiram* (Don't learn the infidel's language; don't go to a Jain temple). How could he worship this English addict of a son-in-law now? The old man sent a message to this effect.

Havilal was already pouring himself into learning English. How could he pass up the chance to do so with the master and the others—to enjoy himself and receive a reward of two or three rupees from time to time,

---
[26] Sharma is a name that can be assumed by any Brahmin.
[27] A title applied to grandfathers or Brahmin men.

whenever he pleased the colonel (and if he pleased him in a grand way)? He might even acquire enough capital to build a house, gleefully turn into a big shot himself, go abroad in a car and become an object of universal envy. So why miss the opportunity? His father-in-law was dumbfounded at his son-in-law's determination to learn English. What could he do if the lad insisted on chewing beaten rice of iron? His protestations bore no fruit.

Havilal, having a good command of Sanskrit and having passed his Matriculation within four years, was slated to leave for studies at Benares University under a government stipend. His special attendance upon the colonel and the others subsided. Caught up in his studies, he could no longer apply himself to currying their particular favour. The latter activity didn't suit him, it may be said.

Havilal got admitted to Benares University. He was accompanied by a cook and a servant. He began to live in a "boarding house." Ah, what a pleasant life it was in the students' hostel! To really enjoy student life, one had to live in one. For one thing, it wasn't at all hard for young adults to hone mental attitudes in a community of students ranging from the undergraduate to master's level. Every hostel had a library with a good number of books and magazines.

From time to time there were discussions during Literary Society meetings between professors and students concerning political and social questions. Pandit Havilal was a good speaker, and once a year the Dramatic Society put on a play. Several times Havilal won the gold medal for his lead role. Western scholars regularly came to visit the university and brightened up student life with words of wisdom.

The youths used to enjoy to the full moonlit nights. It was a spring full moon day. The sky was clear and immaculate—not the least sign of clouds. At about eight in the evening Havilal's closest friend, a fellow named Radheshyam, arrived. "Mr. Sharma, look—the beauty and charm of nature! What a delightful season! First off, it's spring, and a gentle breeze is blowing, but still you insist on being a bookworm rather than plunder the joys of this silver night."

Hearing these words of his friend, Mr. Sharma found himself in a dilemma. Exams were right around the corner, and he had to work hard day and night, but if he begged out there was no telling when he'd get another chance to see such a wondrous natural exhibition.

Nor did the circle of friends enjoy any picnic without Sharma. The latter was swayed by their urgent appeal. They reached Nagowa with all the necessities for a picnic, having taken along a stove and tea with them for a tea party in a boat. Sweets and fruits were also packed away. There was no shortage of harmoniums and tablas. Their evening passed in singing and sporting within the bosom of the river Ganges, the bearer of waters that purify the fallen. Other pleasure-seekers in boats, having their own high time, were delighted to hear them burst out into laughter, sing tender songs and make a ruckus.

Pandit Havilal was in his fourth year. Three years of student life had changed him completely. He had begun to sport dress suits. It took half an hour or an hour to arrange his hair and to smooth half his moustache. His mind was not to be set at ease if he didn't engage in the pleasure of a weekly film. Visiting cards got printed with "Mr. H. L. Sharma" on them. He began to cast contemptuous and scornful looks at uneducated women. The world of his imagination took on a different cast. From time to time he sank into a sea of thought and remembered the rituals and traditional customs of the society in which his whole family had spent their lives. The future had been cloaked in abysmal darkness. Mr. Sharma, having been taken in by the delights of Western civilization, imbued with Western thought and immersed in modern opinion, shivered to think of his home.

What wonder that his thoughts were topsy-turvy! For one thing, he had entered his prime; secondly, the climate of student life was totally opposite to his life back home. He believed the dazzling and beauteous marvels he saw on the stage of an artificial world to be true; he was engrossed in them. At the cinema he saw the laughter and endearments back and forth between English ladies who, at intermission, slipped into a restaurant for some chocolates, biscuits or the like, and went walking in the park snuggled up against their sahibs. In the hostel he saw students affecting the glorified ways of the foreigners. It was natural that all this should turn the head of a youth used to pure Hindu manners. One had to have a strong mind not be tempted by English society. How could Mr. Sharma, who was hooked on English novels, realize that it was best, when acquiring the elements of Western civilization, to throw out the chaff? Thus he fixed on completely different aspirations and felt unease whenever he observed Nepalese social life.

Mr. Sharma went home once a year. His parents and in-laws, noticing the change in his nature, became worried. One day they performed worship for Lord Satyanarayan[28] at home; everybody—close friends, relatives and even neighbours—gathered together. A discussion of Lord Krishna's escapades took place. People were astonished at what Mr. Sharma had to say. The next day the rumour that Chavilal's son had become a Christian started spreading. The discussion had been as follows:

Mr. Sharma—"Our ancestors were very cunning. There may have been a person named Krishna people made a god of. That they blindly followed him and said he was a being of wondrous power to be worshipped is merely benighted tradition."

Pandit Jivanhari—"If we don't worship Krishna, who do we worship? The Supreme Lord, ever ready to relieve his devotees' sufferings, who in Dvarika brought a heap of saris to cover Queen Draupadi's shame during Duryodhana's assembly, who was pleased with the devotion of the poverty-stricken Sudama and so relieved his suffering, who gave the ambrosia of the Gita to Arjuna to drink when he was overwhelmed by delusion during the *Mahabharata*'s terrible battle, set him on his duty's path, and as his charioteer intimately acquainted

---

[28]A name for Vishnu, and at the same time a special worship ceremony conducted for him, usually in the evening, in connection with the fulfilment of some wish.

him with bravery and the art of battle—if we don't worship him, then who?"

An old army officer—"My good sir, why are you talking the way you are? You say it's wrong to worship the Krishna your ancestors have been worshipping all along? What sort of talk is that? And to hear it from the mouth of a Brahmin! Oh, that's Kali-yuga for you!"

Mr. Sharma—"Pandit Jivanhari described Krishna's power; did he see it with his own eyes? He would say this was written down in the *Mahabharata* and *Srimadbhagavat*.[29] If everything in the *Srimadbhagavat* is true, then did Krishna have sixteen thousand cowherdesses as wives?"

Pandit Jivanhari—"No, Babu,[30] you haven't caught on. Nobody can see with their own eyes. The eyes we see with are our sacred writings. When it was said Krishna had sixteen thousand cowherdesses it doesn't mean all were his wives. Krishna was pleased with their devotion and made them so absorbed in him that they saw him as their husband. They loved him. These days, in the Kali-yuga, people see with their outward eyes, and so take everything in the wrong way."

The onlookers' faces brightened up with joy to hear this account of things by Jivanhari. Anxious to know what reply Mr. Sharma would give, everyone now looked at him.

Mr. Sharma—"But Pandit! How old can this *Mahabharata* and *Srimadbhagavat* be? They were written two hundred years ago, I should think. And what proofs are there that everything written in them is true? Do we accept the musings that come out of poetic imagination as something more than they are? No, I don't believe."

Pandit Jivanhari—"Babu, you are running after things on the unconsidered advice of other people, like the bit of childishness of running after a crow after being told it has taken your ear. Don't your Western teachers say that the *Mahabharata* and *Srimadbhagavat* were written long

---

[29] One of the eighteen major Hindu Puranas. It expounds a full-fledged theism centred on the worship of Krishna.

[30] A term of respect or affection for males.

after the birth of Buddha? If that's so, was it false what Megasthenes wrote about Hindus worshipping Krishna and reciting the *Bhagavat* in every house? Your historians regard what he wrote as unshakable. The worship of Krishna has been going on since time immemorial."

Mr. Sharma—"Since there's no historical proof for these things, I'm simply taking a sceptical attitude. No need to get angry."

Pandit Jivanhari—"I'm not angry, Babu. Why is it that these historians who used to cry out that Indian civilization isn't all that ancient have changed their tune after the excavation of Mohenjo-daro and Harappa? It's a fact, Babu! It won't do to be too fastidious."

Pandit Jivanhari had had a good Sanskrit education, and put a modern gloss on his knowledge by reading the latest Hindi magazines. Thus Mr. Sharma was left without anything to say. The pandit's standing solidified; everyone's sympathy was on his side. All were pleased.

Whenever Mr. Sharma came home the same sort of discussions took place in the living room. He couldn't do without tea early in the morning, and biscuits as well. Every day he took a bath, rubbing himself with soap. Twice a day he cleaned his teeth with a toothbrush. The hair he sported was long and curly. He applied scented oil and combed it, and then was ready to go. When he came home he didn't have time to trim even half his moustache; he simply plucked out one or two stray hairs.

৳০৩

Chapter 5

The tribulations faced by Rupamati as a daughter-in-law day in and day out had become intolerable. During the day she had no appetite, and at night no sleep. Both were filled with grumbling and nit-picking. Sometimes the torment became so unbearable that, in her anger, she wanted to jump into Ranipokhari[31] and put an end to all her suffering. But she vividly recalled her father's recitations to her mother from the Puranas during Chaturmas:[32] those who committed suicide would go to the Raurava hell and undergo much pain and torture from mental demons; there she would find no peace, and there would be no end to her suffering. Thus there was no road to happiness but that of tolerating whatever suffering befell her.

Rupamati, just fourteen years old, now had to cook for the whole family. One day villagers from the hills came to inform the cook, Bahunnani,[33] that his mother was seriously ill—a matter of life and death—and insisted that he go home. Rupamati's mother-in-law began to give an angry tilt to her head after cooking just three or four meals. She couldn't let Rupamati cook because only some days before a pebble had been found in the rice, and a fight right out of the *Mahabharata* had taken place. Once the cook had left the house, Rupamati offered her services, but how could her mother-in-law let her cook again after she had said that her daughter-in-law didn't know how to sift rice and was making them chew gravel; her offer would be the death of them.

On that same day Sante's younger sister arrived. She was a servant of Rupamati's parents. She regularly

---

[31] A historic man-made pond in the centre of Kathmandu.
[32] The four months of the year from July-August to October-November when the god Vishnu lies asleep on the serpent Shesha.
[33] A title applied to a young boy Brahmin.

brought food items from Rupamati's mother, which Rupamati in turn passed on to Madam Pandit. That day her mother-in-law was in the kitchen. Khardar[34] Satyaman's daughter had brought some arum *achar*. A conversation with her was in progress. As soon as the matron heard that somebody had come from Rupamati's parents, she began to wax sarcastical. "Look, Nanicha![35] What a Kali-yuga in my house! All day long she lolls about like a guest; morning and evening fattens up on food others have cooked and sits around like a fool— that's all. Who could tolerate such awful behaviour from a daughter-in-law? Really, I'm so fed up. How can she clean out the pantry come lunch and dinner? When she eats, three *manas*[36] is not enough for her. And on top of that she has a taste for delicacies: not a bite without some curry."

Nanicha looked at the speaker with surprise, interjecting a "Yes, Bajyai" now and then—enough to please the old lady. Rupamati was astonished to hear such piercing words. Any response would have backfired: the volume of her mother-in-law's voice would have skyrocketed. It would be like adding oil to fire. But if she didn't respond, what would the servant think? What would she tell her mother? Poor Rupamati was in a great dilemma, but she endured all and kept mum. From that evening on Rupamati took the responsibility for cooking. People stopped wondering about when Bahunnani would come back, nor was there any talk of taking turns. For the old woman it was the end of the world to have to cook even the four days when Rupamati had her period.

Since that day Rupamati had had no time even to breathe. From dawn to the sound of the cannon at night the engine that kept Rupamati going never stopped. She never found time to rest. But however tasty her cooking might be, it reaped no praise. If the curry was ever so

---

[34]The second-highest rank among non-gazetted staff in the civil service.

[35]A term of address to girls and junior women in the Newari language.

[36]1 *mana* = 0.568 l.

oily, she was accused of daring to ruin the meal with gobs of ghee and oodles of oil, on the principle that it's the sponsor, not the priest, who pays for the rites; she hadn't had to spend her father's money. The old woman made things insufferable for her: If there was too little oil, she suspected Rupamati of having simply boiled the vegetables, even though four *dharnis*[37] of ghee and eight *kuruvas*[38] of oil a month was not enough for her. Yet when it came time to eat, the food was always the same old fare. She lost quantities of oil to spillage, and finished off other large amounts to cook something for her father. Rupamati was so careless. She got on people's nerves— what a choice for a bride! No manners, no conscientiousness. Rupamati was used to hearing all this, but coming from a good family she never opened her mouth. She took on a sombre look and held her anger in check.

Ravilal was also growing up. Madam Pandit wished to see him married. The search for a bride began. None of their intimate friends could come up with one that fit their specifications. It wasn't that Ravilal was a bumbling idiot. He was studying in the school for civil service candidates, having completed the forty-chapter course of study of the Veda. He had taken the second-level examination. Why didn't people come forward to offer their daughter to such a groom? It wasn't that they needed to wonder where the next meal would come from, so how come this sorry state of affairs? It was all due to Madam Pandit's contrary nature. No one wished to push their own daughter into a fire. The pandit began to get nervous.

It was then that news of a prospective bride came from Chepetar. The Barals of that place, within the past thirty to forty years, had attained to great prosperity. The prospective bride's grandfather, Shishupal Baral, had inherited his sonless father-in-law's wealth, accumulated from a dairy the latter had set up in Burma. He had invested this wealth within the village. Living expenses were met from the interest earned on the money. By now

---

[37] 1 *dharni* = 2.2 kg.
[38] 1 *kuruva* = 2 *manas* = 1.136 l.

he had also amassed much land. They lived to show off their wealth, and accounted to no others the station of man. Very proud of their riches they were. To the would-be father-in-law the black letters of the alphabet were like black buffaloes.[39] He used to boast of his illiteracy that it kept him from having to earn his keep from priestly duties. He used to strut about—a cigarette clamped in his mouth and a thin walking stick in hand—wearing red socks, black shoes, alpaca attire from which hung a watch chain, and an embroidered cap worn at a cock, and so tried to make a splash. But he had not the temperament for conversation. He knew not what manner of thing respect and good behaviour was, and how to talk at a gathering of four persons. If he tried to converse spit bubbled out of his mouth. It was decided to marry Ravilal Sharma to the daughter of this same pandit, Madhuvan Baral. The bridegroom's father was taken in by their show.

Mr. Sharma came home during this time, having completed his B.A. examination. Preparations for the marriage were under way. Neighbours, friends and relatives gathered to help Madam Pandit with the work. Some were busy making leaf-plates, others were husking gram, and still others were preparing *achar*; a pleasant atmosphere prevailed. The day came when they all left, except for the old woman's favourites—Dahalni Bajyai and Dhai Budhi,[40] the wet-nurse. They, too, were hurrying to leave, but the old woman held them back. Once the *sel*, flat-bread and curds were set down in front of them, though, talk got going.

Madam Pandit—"Did you notice my sister-in-law[41] today? She really put her daughter-in-law in her place. She's just a child, and naturally gets tired working. Why should she shout at her for looking from the window awhile?"

Dhai Budhi—"It's useless to talk about your sister-in-law. Day and night she grumbles and grouses with her

---

[39] A proverb in Nepali descriptive of an uneducated state.
[40] A *dhai* is a wet-nurse, and *budhi* a title applied to old women.
[41] Her husband's elder sister.

daughter-in-law. Praised be the daughter-in-law! She never uttered a word."

Dahalni Bajyai—"Poor girl! I hope she gets enough to eat in spite of such rebukes. The amount of rice they give her to cook is a fixed quota. The poor thing always ends up with only half her stomach filled."

Madam Pandit—"What's the use of letting the money moulder? Is she planning to take it with her when she dies?"

Dahalni Bajyai—"She's the type to recover with her teeth a coin that drops down the drain. Nobody would expect her to give away money, no matter what the need."

Dhai Budhi—"She doesn't have the kind heart your good self has, Bajyai; it must have been lotted from your previous birth—being able to give and feed. I pierced her grandson's ear. Do you know how much I got for it? Just one rupee. What's the point in having so much wealth?"

Madam Pandit—"Why were our brother-in-law's[42] daughters-in-law so mannerless? They have absolutely no shame."

Dhai Budhi—"They're in the full bloom of youth and have stopped using their eyes to see."

Madam Pandit—"We also went through youth, but no one could call us insolent."

Dhai Budhi—"A good, upstanding family is what's needed, Bajyai! You know what they say: 'Water from the source, a daughter from a good family.' Yours is an entirely different case."

Dahalni Bajyai—"I've never seen a well-mannered person to match you. That's why you can handle the responsibility of running such a big house."

Madam Pandit was delighted. She offered them each two more *barphi*s and another *jilebi*.

Madam Pandit—"No, I'll tell you. Our brother-in-law's wife is strange—the sort that can't put up with daughters-in-law at all. At Dasain she should have given them outfits and something nice to go along with them. What she bought must be calico."

---

[42]Her husband's younger brother.

Dhai Budhi—"That's why the daughters-in-law were so sad. She never talks sweetly with them. She's always keeping a tight rein over them."

Dahalni Bajyai—"Daughters-in-law must be made to toe the line as much as possible; otherwise they don't regard mothers-in-law as humans. So said your sister-in-law. Your sister-in-law is a true sister-in-law."

Dhai Budhi—"I've never seen any religious donations being given in their house—not one paisa. They don't have good food even during festivals. What do they do, I wonder? Where are they putting so much cheaply earned money?"

Dahalni Bajyai—"And why does your sister-in-law so often need to poke around in other people's business? She spends the whole day talking about others."

Madam Pandit—"I, too, was astonished at how many stories she could tell about people. As if she can't digest her food without talking about others. It's awful. As for us, we don't even know how to talk, and don't sit around either talking about others' business. There's no time to breathe for all the housework."

Dhai Budhi—"How could every house have a Lakshmi like you, Bajyai?"

Dahalni Bajyai—"Where's a graceful person like you to be found?"

Three or fours days after this talk each of them got one outfit on the occasion of Ravilal's wedding.

A long discussion was also held on how many outfits were to be presented to the bride. Mr. Sharma said, "Three outfits is enough. It'll be better to provide clothes as they're needed, once the bride has settled in with us. Why the unnecessary expenditure?"

The old woman began to shout. "Eleven outfits were given to the bride of Raghupati's son. What will people say if we give less?"

"Let others do what they want. And what about her? She worked as a wet-nurse in the palace and collected many clothes. Such unnecessary expenditures are not good." Mr. Sharma pressed his point, but it didn't go over. All the women gathered there came back at him with some direct words, saying that nine outfits had been given to the bride at his own marriage, so why this preaching now?

There were a goodly number of people in the wedding procession of Ravilal. The bride was quartered in Battisputali. The Barals were not lacking in money. Those who came in the procession were channelled off into different meal lines. They were served with two handfuls of beaten rice, two twisted *sels*, burnt *rotis*, two helpings of *kasar*,[43] a bit of fermented radish, some relish and pea *achar*. Madhuvan Baral looked inviolable that day. His nattiness—the twist in his moustache, his manner of talking—could be taken as unmistakable tokens of his sense of superiority. Those who came expecting to enjoy some good food at a rich man's place, though, were sorely disappointed.

After the ritual held for the groom, Madhuvan came to pay his respects to the groom's party. "What to do away from home? I thought of honouring you all in a grand manner. I even ordered goats from the Terai, but they didn't arrive," he said, twiddling his moustache.

The bride was so-so. Her lips were a bit thick, one tooth was a little crooked, and her nose was long. Her mother-in-law welcomed her into the home. But could the group of women who were critical of Rupamati be expected to sit still? "What good is a hill Brahmin's daughter? Why is she so sombre?" "She looked downright ugly when she smiled." "Why are her eyes so beady?" Such were their criticisms. But Madam Pandit could barely keep her feet on the ground, she was so happy. Who can match the delight of parents-in-law on a wedding day? So overjoyed they are at the arrival of the bride that other people's faces blur.

☙❧

---

[43] A typical Nepalese sweet prepared for weddings, made from grains of rice fried in ghee, cooked in sugarcane juice and formed into hard balls.

Chapter 6

The Nepal family's happiness knew no bounds when news of the success of Mr. Sharma in securing first division marks in his B.A. reached them. And why not? Their son's endeavours had paid off, and on top of that it was no easy matter to be first class. His friends who had honied tongues but hearts of gall soothed their envy with random comments. In their opinion such a miraculous performance at the Hindu University did not go down as a miracle; it was child's play.

Preparations began for Mr. Sharma to go for M.A. studies. Having a bent for English literature, he decided to major in that subject. He had been awarded gold medals by the university many a time for his essays. He took interest in composing poems and showed no little skill in writing short stories. A person of his calibre was advised to continue on.

Mr. Sharma was inclined to do so, but he was turned off by the customs and traditions of his home. He hardly agreed on anything with anybody. He used to tell his family to prepare the morning and evening meals on schedule. As things stood, though, a host of festivals, fasting periods and worship were always taking place. Nothing happened at a fixed time. He constantly got upset to see the rules of hygiene being broken. He had no sense for the importance of religion in their lives. If faced with an unexpected period of mourning, they had to purify themselves by restricting their diet to the *panchagavya*.[44] The thought of drinking cow's urine caused pain only death could have relieved. He pretended to imbibe it and, when no one was looking, poured it out. He could not see eye to eye with his parents. How could he, who had

---

[44]The five sacred substances produced by a cow: milk, curds, ghee, dung and urine.

steeped himself in modern ways, take delight in his elders' traditional modes of thought? Even Rupamati knew not how to please him. For one thing, her mother-in-law had filled ears with false stories about her; secondly, he was put off by the sight of her habits, attire, ideas of cleanliness and the like. Remembering vividly life in a university hostel, he took a dim view of life at home.

Pandit Chavilal and his wife were deeply saddened by their son's behaviour. They never complained, hoping that he, being their clever eldest son, and educated to boot, would look after them in their old age. They never raised any ticklish questions, thinking that they might thereby hurt him. Poor Rupamati had to work like a donkey, so she never had time to spruce up and beautify herself to please her husband, though she wasn't the sort to go in for affectation in the first place. Her only aid was her own gentle nature and her own natural beauty.

Thus, if her husband was happy with her, he was happy, and if not, she had to make do with blaming her own lot. There were enough reasons for Rupamati to be disheartened. One day she heard some whispering going on between mother and son.

Mother—"Really, Havi, I don't see any household in the future with the wife you've got. She's lacking something. Her parents went overboard in pampering her as an only child. How can the house run with her the way she is? If I ask her one thing she comes back with seven answers. If I try to explain to her not to do that, she puts on a long face. These days, since you came home, I see she's been keeping quite active."

The heroines of novels and films were swirling about in the son's head; how could he take pleasure in his innocent gentle wife? He chimed in with his mother, and the old woman went into higher gear. "Yes, Havi, we're long into old age, and there's no getting around the fact that the whole responsibility for running the house will lie on your wife's shoulders. Our younger daughter-in-law is just a new bride, so what can I say to her? If the elder daughter-in-law is good, the younger ones will also be good. Dahalni Bajyai used to say that the daughter of the Kaphtes from Bhaimal was a real Lakshmi.[45] Should we negotiate a marriage with her?"[46]

Mr. Sharma—"What are you talking about, Mother? Isn't one rustic fool enough for you that you're keen on another one? Why invite a headache by tying your head in a noose?"

The mother felt as if she had toppled from the roof when the son refused to marry a second time. She became suspicious that Rupamati secretly pleased him. Noticing his mother's gloomy face, he instantly understood, and said, "I see her face and my blood boils. I really feel duped now, having married such a low creature. If we have this painful problem to put up with from one wife, imagine the distress if we brought another one?"

Madam Pandit's breast swelled with pleasure. She began to speak at full volume. "Are all people the same?"

Mr. Sharma was quick to deny.

From this conversation Rupamati became convinced that she could not please her husband. However, she was beautiful and of a gentle nature. She consoled herself as best she could by remembering the proverb, "The river comes back to itself after twelve years." Her husband's good graces would surely return; why shouldn't they?

Preparations for Mr. Sharma's departure for Benares had begun. He had already said good-bye to everyone. The only reason he was still around was because his cook had not come from the hills. He had a strong desire to plunge into life's battle after finishing his M.A. But *"Mama ichchha samo nasti daiva ichchha baliyasi"*;[47] who had the power to understand God's will? Men get caught up in their imaginations and build castles in the air, thinking to achieve this and that, but when struck by an ill star, they're jolted back to their senses. For a while they keep the lesson in mind, but then redescend into delusion. This is the way of the world.

---

[45]The name of the Hindu goddess of wealth is applied to women who have a good nature and bring good luck.

[46]At the time the story takes place, a man could marry as many wives as he wanted.

[47]The Sanskrit equivalent of "Man proposes, God disposes."

A cholera epidemic spread far and wide. In the month of Asar[48] water had to be boiled before drinking it; food that had sat around could not be eaten. Flies needed to be kept away from it. Sweets from the open market, for example, on which flies freely landed, could not be consumed. Mr. Sharma regularly discoursed about the need to wash pots and pans with potash; raw vegetables—everything in fact—had to be washed with potash. All this was mandatory for him; otherwise he wouldn't eat. But his father Pandit Chavilal Nepal was totally deaf to such talk; he would dismiss it as a joke. What is lotted cannot be blotted, he would say, so why all the fuss?

One day a frightening disease befell him. Doctors, both modern and traditional, gathered about. He barely held on, and that only thanks to injections. The old man was scared witless at having come down with cholera at his age. All his stamina went out of him. His life force was spent. In fact, he couldn't keep his head raised.

Everyone advised Mr. Sharma not to go off and leave his father in that condition. His father could hardly move his hands and legs, and if he for his part didn't move into action quickly, they'd have nothing to eat. The great problem of filling stomachs loomed. It wouldn't be proper to keep on sending his father to Battisputali. His father hadn't the energy to walk. The only way out was to go himself to the colonel; his family had at all costs to be taken care of.

Mr. Sharma's courage flagged. His heart's desire, to show his manhood by obtaining an M.A., melted away entirely. His mother's grumbling was becoming all the worse—the more so, the more she noticed their income decreasing. He was beset by worry, wondering what would happen next. From time to time he saw the writing on the wall: he would have to find some source of income.

The weaker old Chavilal got, the more irritable he became, exploding over trifles. The younger brother, Ravilal, was just entering into full youth and hardly cared about anyone. He spent his time from morning to ten

---

[48] June-July.

o'clock at night in the company of rowdy drug addicts. Sometimes, just to throw dust in the eyes of his family, he went through the motions of going to accountancy school. The cook had to be sent out looking for him at lunch and dinner time. There was not a single day the food didn't have to wait. Nobody dared utter a word; his thunderings would have been loud. He put wrong twists on straightforward matters. Any advice not to keep bad company was poison to him. If his mother tried to reason with him by saying, "Why do you make me cry this way, my son? How will you support your wife and children in the future? Older brothers won't be around to help forever; have you seen how your sister-in-law is?", he replied, "Mother, don't get on my back. Take it easy. If we've gone bad, it's all right. Let us do what we want."

He wasn't earning a paisa, but who would know it from his ostentation? He felt compelled to go about decked out with an embroidered cap, a chain around his neck, a woollen coat, a select pair of muslin trousers laced at the ankles, a silk shirt, the latest fashion in shoes, Japanese silk socks, a patterned handkerchief in his coat pocket, a West End watch on his wrist, a tuft of curly hair and a flower the size of a lotus leaf stuck into the buttonhole of his coat. All these were to be provided by his home. If they didn't materialize, such a stink was raised that everyone got the shivers.

He usually managed to extract the money he needed from his mother. The woman had a soft spot in her heart! If she didn't give when asked, he said he would go jump into Ranipokhari, whereupon a trickle of sweat began to flow. She took his threat for real and came up with the sum.

Thus Ravilal's temperament went from bad to worse by the day. Now he had gradually begun to acquire a zeal for gambling. In every respect Mr. Sharma saw black. It was natural for him to be overcome with hopelessness at knowing himself to be a young man with no business experience who had been forcibly driven from his dormitory into life's battle at the helm of the whole house.

Rupamati seemed to be a star that brought relief with its bit of light for the pilgrims disoriented by the thick new moon darkness in Mr. Sharma's home. Seeing her strenuous labours gradually had an effect on her husband's heart. A heart of iron would have melted at one frail woman who, besides all the domestic chores, overlooked nothing in attending to her sickly father-in-law, tolerated the gratuitous scoldings of her mother-in-law, always bore up under everything with a bright disposition, and stuck to her job day and night. Why would the heart of the educated Mr. Sharma have felt a different effect?

It became difficult to support the growing family on the income from the colonel. Mr. Sharma hunted all over creation for a job. His friends all thought teaching in a school best for him, but he didn't feel any particular interest in that direction. His great desire was to find a post in any office where he would have to use his brain in some studious pursuit, and so lead a meaningful life in faithful service to government and nation. This was his prayer day and night. And indeed within one or two months he got appointed to the Kausal[49] and started working with heart and soul. The family's distress at what it would eat or wear ceased. Madam Pandit also calmed down somewhat.

Pandit Chavilal, too, began to spend most of his time at home. When he felt a bit energetic, he went to Battisputali three days in a row, even though his son tried his best to persuade him that this was the wistfulness of old age. He suffered a recurrence of gout. For days he had not the strength to walk. A plaything of the gods, he was unable to get back on his feet once stricken.

One day the old man was late in rising. Rupamati prepared the daily decoction and was conscientiously set on making him take it. Since he hadn't risen, she sent Chameli to look in on him. Chameli came back upstairs terrified and said, "Madam, your father-in-law is lying stretched out flat. I called to him, but he didn't answer. I thought he might be sleeping, but when he sleeps he snores. Today he's not snoring, so I went up and nudged him, but no reaction."

---

[49]The government accounting office during the Rana period.

Rupamati's expression changed; her face fell. She was downstairs in a breath. She looked at him; he was already very dead. No one had noticed that the old man had taken the road to heaven, leaving behind his transient body. Seeing what was before her, Rupamati let out a shriek and began to cry. At that, Chameli, too, began to wail and moan. The old woman was in the prayer-room. She came running down, wondering what had happened? She saw the dead body of her husband and fell to the floor.

A clamorous lamentation arose. In the meantime Mr. Sharma came back from his morning walk, and Ravilal, though high on hashish at his hideout, also came, upon hearing the uproar at home. The neighbours gathered. As soon as Mr. Sharma knew what had happened he brought the dead body downstairs with the help of three or four Brahmins. He was taken to the byre, and offerings were made. Babucha[50] went to call the priest.

Hearing the tidings, the latter said, "Ah me, the poor man is gone, and an honest old man he was. Ram! Ram! Ram! What sad news you've brought, Babucha!" And off he ran to his client's house to perform the rituals.

Mr. Sharma fell into a state of unbearable wretchedness at this stroke of fate. What constellation of the planets had dashed his hopes of studying for an M.A. and now delivered this blow to him after he had barely set foot in his new office? Mr. Sharma had previously never believed in the stars—not even in the slightest. It is only when misfortune strikes that men take note, and so it was that the notion that the movements of heavenly bodies could have a great effect on human life gradually gained credence with him.

Dahalni Bajyai, Dhai Budhi and Jite's mother—everyone gathered to console the old lady. Dahalni Bajyai came up the stairs babbling away in her sobs, but not a word of it could be understood. She said, "Where has my pandit gone? How he used to love me! Whenever festivals came he used to address me as madam and put some rupees in my hand. If he heard I was sick he came personally to

---

[50]The name of the Newar servant.

look after me. Now who will take pity on me? Why did death take him instead of an old woman like me? Oh Lordie, if only you had been quick to pluck me away, my eyes wouldn't have had to witness this misfortune!"

She was both speaking and shedding tears simultaneously. The other matrons had begun consoling the widow, and at first Dahalni Bajyai did not notice this. She began to wail louder than the widow. It was quite a spectacle. Dahalni Bajyai started in babbling again. "Madam Pandit, what's wrong with you? Why should you be crying? You have a jewel of a son. But look at my condition! How my son did please his master—couldn't be a single moment without him. If he missed showing up even a day, a man was sent for him immediately. There was no need to complain about not having things for festivals. But without warning fate took him away. How do you think I got over that? My younger son was brilliant. He came in first in Sanskrit. He passed the examination here, and went and began studying in Benares. You can imagine what a blow it was for us when we heard of his death there. Two such sons have left me, and my husband has too. We're left to console ourselves. What's going on around us? Whatever happens, we must plod on. Today our loving pandit has gone to heaven, and we must bear up. The day Pandit was confined to bed with gout my heart stopped beating. And dreams—my word! For the last few days I haven't had a single good one. That such things should happen!"

Everyone seconded what Dahalni Bajyai said.

Dhai Budhi—"Madam, where will we find another such godlike pandit? What to do? He left us so suddenly. We've become orphans. But what do you have to worry about? You have worthy and qualified sons, come what may."

Jite's mother—"My fortune has sunk, Madam! Saturn has come around again,[51] so what good can you expect? Only the other day Pandit showed great kindness to me:

---

[51] The poor configuration of Saturn occurs in one's horoscope every seven years.

'Now don't worry', he said, 'my son said that he'd get your son set up as a soldier.' Oh, how much he loved us!"

"Why did you go, leaving me behind? Why didn't death come to me? What am I to do now?" Madam Pandit intoned, and began to cry. In between she also listened to what the others were saying. Mr. Sharma had already taken the dead body down. The old lady began to make motions in front of the window as if about to jump from it.

All the old women present had a hard time attending to her. The old ladies gradually lessened the pangs of sorrow. Death—how dreadful it is! It's death that makes away with man's life; death that snuffs out sons and daughters, and leaves a mordant wound in the breast of their parents; death that at a stroke causes unbearable pain, bereaving either a husband or a wife who was caught up in the transports of marriage; and the same death, too, that gradually lessens the pain of the wound. The medicine for death is death itself. The consolation of close friends reduces the pangs of grief at death from twenty to nineteen, but the truly invaluable medicine for this grief is death. Were it not so, by now the world would have been filled with the cries of its sufferers. The normal course of life would not have proceeded.

The passing of days brought an easing of grief for the Nepal family. Their clever Lamsal priest's energy and vigour went on attaining new heights. He brought a prepared list of things needed for the mourning ritual on the eleventh day following death. Shopping started. The priest placed special orders, and his close friends also told the old lady that if she didn't offer a silver bowl and one or two gold ornaments to him, people would gossip. Mr. Sharma heard about how the priest's wife was saying that things had to be done with some style now that he had a job high up. But he was well read; he uttered not a word and pretended not to hear anything. He performed all the rituals faithfully, in the way they were supposed to be, and was absolved from the debt owed to ancestors. For some days his separation from the father who begot him weighed on his mind. But as the whole ceremony unfolded the grief gradually faded away. Only the memory remained. The time had come for Mr. Sharma to enter into life's struggle.

༺༻

Chapter 7

After three or four days of mourning for Pandit Chavilal a conversation occurred in the house of the son of the pandit's uncle between two old ladies and the mistress of the household.

Nandu's mother from next door—"No, the old man died in his bed, they say, wasn't it, Dulahi?[52] How could they offer any religious gifts.[53] How unfortunate for the old man, Dulahi Bajyai! The son was very clever; he took the dead body to the byre and pretended to give an offering to the priest. He died so suddenly, how could they give an offering? What use pretending after death?"

Gharteni Budhi from the other side of the hill—"No, Bajyai, they say the body was a bit warm."

Nandu's mother—"Nonsense! Was he still breathing? It was useless display! Last year when Dulahi Bajyai went to see Indrajatra,[54] I thought something bad was sure to happen in the house. How can things go right when quarrels take place day and night?"

Gharteni Budhi—"Yes, Bajyai! Madam's elder sister-in-law is contemptible! How can any good come from constant teeth-gnashing?"

Nandu's mother—"She must have realized the daughter-in-law she torments day and night wants to take charge of things. You know the saying, 'Parents' love is for their children; children's love is for rocks.'"

Dulahi Bajyai—"Now we'll see what she's made of. That's why they say people should not be proud. The poor old man used to try to talk sense into her. Well meaning

---

[52] A title applied to a daughter-in-law in the household.

[53] It is inauspicious in Hindu culture to die in bed. A dying person should at least be taken downstairs, if not to the ghats.

[54] A festival celebrated during a week in August-September towards the end of the monsoon in honour of Indra, the rain god, and Kumari, the living goddess.

words were poison for her. For as long as he lived the old man never could raise his head. Do you think he got any rest after coming back home from a hard day's work? If he had, he would have been more active on the job. His worries would have been less. The old man was sick of all the quarrelling day and night. I often heard him thinking out loud with my own ears that he should rub ashes on his body and leave home; he didn't see any use in looking after such a house."

Gharteni Budhi—"Yes, Dulahi Bajyai, you're right. She couldn't be happy unless tasting the sin of making the old man cry, Bajyai."

Nandu's mother—"No, and why were the offerings on the eleventh day what they were? So rich and just offering brass plates, I heard. Couldn't they afford even an alloy of brass and bronze?"

While the conversation was going on Pandit Bichi Nepal arrived and began listening.

Dulahi Bajyai—"Did you say plates? What among all their collection looked good? Nothing looked decent, I heard. For the set of dishes given to the younger daughter-in-law as a dowry they got old ware from roaming pot traders. That's why the family priest looked discontented. Didn't you notice? He looked so sad. They say it's not good when the family priest is hurt."

Bichi didn't feel right not saying anything, and immediately he replied, "Okay, it's not good to hurt the priest, but what about his client? Was it right to grab those sons by the neck two days after their father dies and tell them they have to offer silver plates, that the weight of the gold image must not be less than a *tola*,[55] that nothing should be less than the best for the eleventh day, and on and on? That's why the custom of offering is declining."

Nandu's mother—"Not so, young fellow! What's the family priest to do? If he had got a big sum before, he wouldn't have had to set his sights on the death rituals. What hope can the priest have when they're tightfisted on auspicious occasions? Haven't you seen how our client

---

[55] 1 *tola* = 11.66 grams.

captain, Julum Bahadur, goes about things? For the whole year the income from him isn't even twenty rupees."

Bichi—"That too lies with the priest. First the priest must be devoted; he must possess the power to rouse faith in his client by his own holy life; he must perform the worship in his client's house properly, for their well being. Taking time to recite and perform worship carefully so that nothing gets left out—that wins people's hearts. What are clients to do when priests flip through the pages they're reciting and click their prayer-beads off lickety-split? What can Julum Bahadur do? Your son can't recite the *Chandi*,[56] yet he goes on performing all the rituals. How can he create belief in his performance? First we should reform ourselves. Then only should we criticize. We don't see the buffalo on our own body; it's the lice on others' bodies we see."

What could the women say to that? They all remained silent. Bichi got himself even more worked up and said, "What in blazes has got into the heads of priests? People wouldn't feel bad if they were criticized for not giving enough on auspicious occasions, but they're not. When tragedy strikes—it's then they're taunted, and you can imagine how terrible they must feel. A wound at that time will never heal."

This time everyone agreed with what he said. Now there was no need for him to speak. The reason Bichi Nepal took his uncle's grandsons under his wings wasn't that he sympathized with them. The words Chattu had uttered at his father's death still gnawed at him, and since that day his faith in his priest had been on the decline.

Talk of the death of Mr. Sharma's father was also going on in the house of Jethi Sasu.[57] Four or five women were in on it.

Jethi Sasu—"The old man may have been simple and gentle, but how could he have passed away in bed? No cow was given—nothing was performed."

---

[56] The praise of the goddess Durga recited during the Dasain festival.

[57] A name and form of address for a wife's elder sister or certain other more distant female relations on the wife's side. The text makes it clear that here the latter is the case.

Haribadan—"'The mouth says "Ram! Ram!" The stomach does a butcher's work.' From the outside things looked nice; inside there were a hundred layers of filth."

Jayanti—"There's no one at the colonel's place who's not offended by him, but nobody dared to utter a word. He distorted what they said against them. If anyone made a simple comment, he twisted a hundred totally different meanings out of them. Blowing things out of proportion and sticking it to you—that was his nature."

Jethi Sasu—"The colonel couldn't do without him for a moment. How did such a person get into his good graces?"

Haribadan—"I myself used to be a wet-nurse there, Bajyai! I know everything. Why shouldn't the colonel have been pleased with him? Four loads of grass were needed for the barn every day? Well, he had the herdsmen cut it. If anyone came an hour late he was marked absent. If four annas'[58] worth of leaves were needed, he himself went to Indrachowk from Battisputali. He gave his master to believe that none of his servants were trustworthy; that everyone was stealing food from him. The colonel used to say that if he had three other servants like Chwanke,[59] he wouldn't have to look after the house; what could he do alone, though?"

Jayanti—"You'll not find a bigger penny pincher than him. He was as slick as they come—deducting two rupees from a monthly salary of five from the gatekeeper for being absent, or giving just seven annas instead of eight to a day labourer for cheating them. He got in good with his master by making everyone else cry, but what's the use of making a profit on potatoes and radishes? Some people the colonel lent twenty thousand to were lying around doing nothing; not a paisa had been paid back. The police seized them and brought them to his house. They were kept on the ground floor for two or three days under lock and key and put through the wringer, but then they huddled together with Chwanke and got off the hook. One got a loan of five thousand rupees by putting

---

[58] 1 anna = 4 paisa.
[59] A nickname for Chavilal, meaning one whose teeth are irregular.

up his home and land as collateral. A case was filed in court, and when the document was studied, it was found that Chwanke had fiddled with it. How disgraced the colonel must have felt after losing the case! With the paddy and other stuff going totally to rot in the granary, what's the use of outward show?"

Jethi Sasu—"It wasn't that way all the time. Of course, all servants should have their master's interest at heart. What's the good of it if you just need small things and then ruin your master by not paying attention to what counts? You're doomed with such a person working for you."

Haribadan—"Chwanke filled his own stomach, and how! He managed to acquire land and a house thanks to his post. How he did was a surprise to everyone."

Poor Chavilal had no peace even after death. Much talk about him went on for a month or two. Little by little his death made everyone tone down. Mr. Sharma, too, began taking full responsibility for the house and its smooth running. Baral's daughter, for her part, came back to observe the mourning period of her father-in-law.

☙☙

Chapter 8

Baral's daughter entered into Chavilal's home deciding to mourn her father-in-law's death there itself. What a chore it had been for Madam Pandit to bring one daughter-in-law under control. Now another had come along. Luintel's wife had trained her daughter in all the niceties, yet the latter had become an eyesore for Madam Pandit. Baral's daughter had come straight from the hills thoroughly spoiled (her feet had not touched the ground for all her family's wealth), and there was something peculiar about her. Thinking she might have trouble all by herself, Madhuvan Baral had sent Batuli along with her. Batuli looked to be of the same age, but she was much more combustible.

Even though Baral's daughter had reached thirteen, she still was small. Her front teeth were somewhat more out of kilter than they had once been, so that when she laughed part of her gums could be seen. There was no charm to either her smile or her talk. She knew nothing about respect. Sometimes when her brother-in-law and mother-in-law got together to discuss something, she would stand still and listen. If any newcomers paid a visit, she stood staring at them. If she laughed on the top floor of the house, it could be heard down in the living room. When no one was looking, she would take *achar* from the jar, and if she came up empty-handed, one or two mouthfuls of ghee vanished. The number of sweets lessened in the twinkling of an eye. She went out of her way to talk with her husband and brother-in-law, but she couldn't stand the sight of her sister-in-law, such was her pride in her wealth. It was difficult for Madam Pandit to keep Baral's daughter under control.

It had to be said that peace prevailed for five or six days after Baral's daughter's return, even though Rupamati had been rebuked from time to time. There was, however, a little less of this than before. Mr. Sharma noticed how she always put her heart into work without paying heed to her mother-in-law's grumblings, and he began to feel affection and compassion for her.

He was seeing his own dreams fade away as a result of being increasingly enmeshed in the affairs of this world. Beautiful women in novels ceased to work their charms on him; he had only the feeling they might once have done so. At the sight of Rupamati's burgeoning youth, a current of love coursed through his whole body. Her youthfulness was like the blooming of a rose, a flash of light invested her smile, and her eyebrow looked like a black snake flowing along in the depths of the Ganges. He on whom her large eyes fell felt a tingle. Beauty had taken up station in her, and royally so. And the character of this young belle was of the same nature. Friends and relatives all felt tinges of anger and envy at seeing Mr. Sharma's good fortune. To obtain such a goddess of a wife, one would have had to engage in strict penances in a previous life. It's not that beautiful women are not to be found; they are. But the two qualities, beauty and a good nature, are combined in few women—a fact of life everyone will acclaim. Praise be to you, O Lord! That a jewel of a woman with both should have lived in the same house as a spiteful woman without either is all a part of your sport!

The forty-fifth day[60] following the death of Chavilal was coming up. Friends and neighbours gathered to offer help. A husband's love had performed an elixir's work on Rupamati. She who had been hard pressed by her mother-in-law's excesses and impetuosities was now determined not to succumb to gloom and let hopelessness overwhelm her, but rather to keep the household going. Her sense of mission was growing steadily. She it was who welcomed the visitors with respect, she who kept tabs on who had not eaten after a whole day's work.

---

[60] A day on which a deceased relative is remembered with a special ritual.

Noticing her son's love for her daughter-in-law rise somewhat, Madam Pandit tempered her anger towards her. The real reason for her decreased anger was a different one, though. She had discovered a world of difference between Baral's daughter and Rupamati. She began to notice that all the imaginary bad qualities she used to mention to her husband and son with regard to the latter were actually present in the younger daughter-in-law. When seven or eight women sat down to work the younger daughter-in-law came downstairs noisily, jostled her way to the centre of things and plopped herself down.

That day she looked different. Limitless quantities of powder had been dabbed all over her face, lipstick applied to her lips, hair clips stuck randomly throughout her locks, strong scented oil smeared to the dripping point on her hair, and lavender perfume sprayed indiscriminately. Upon witnessing this, the women present looked at one another. That day, too, she flaunted clothes brought from her parents. A patterned alpaca sari, a muslin bodice and a *tarchin*[61] shawl added splendour to her physique. The sleeves of the bodice were a bit long; the ends were not joined in the middle, and something of her body could be seen beneath the shawl. In addition, she was decked out in ornaments, and had veiled her head.

As soon as she came and sat down, she launched into talk without any thought to doing work. She had close ties to the neighbour Banshi Pathak's daughter. Pretending that she was talking to her, she in fact began to address everyone. "Let me tell you, Didi,[62] we never lacked anything at my parents' place. Cows gave milk the whole year—cans full of it you couldn't finish! Milk and buttermilk had to be thrown out. My father never touched the rice unless it was dripping with ghee. We had hordes of debtors; they brought wicker baskets full of walnut leaves and didn't know where to put them all. No

---

[61] A cloth embroidered with threads of gold, silver and copper.

[62] A form of address applied to elder sisters and any woman elder to oneself.

one could have eaten all the bananas, guavas and jack-fruits!"

Her friend continuously seconded everything she said. She affected great interest, and having heard everything she said, "Well, if so, will you take me with you when you go to your parents' next time?"

"Okay, why not? Come along once, then you'll be hooked."

Chameli filled the mother-in-law's ears with how her younger daughter-in-law had boastfully extolled herself and disturbed the ritual work. Madam Pandit arrived on the scene mumbling.

Seeing her daughter-in-law's getup and hearing her glibness of tongue, she froze. For a while no words came from her, but then her head caught fire, and she began to speak heatedly. "What blind idiots arranged the marriage of such as floozy for my son? The day after tomorrow is the forty-fifth day of my husband's death. Where would we be if Dhai Budhi, Dahalni Bajyai and you others hadn't come to help? My hands have stopped functioning; I hardly know what's going on around me. Yesterday my elder son asked me for the key to a box. I searched all over creation and couldn't find it. Then I asked my elder daughter-in-law. She said, 'It's hanging from the strap of your bodice.' When I looked, it really was hanging there. I've lost my senses. What's my elder daughter-in-law to do by herself?"

Then, turning towards her younger daughter-in-law: "How can someone who doesn't lift a finger to do anything be so dressy? She wouldn't break a toothpick if you wanted her to; and if her hands aren't any good, she should shut up. She's only out to disturb others doing their work."

The girl had no chance to speak; it was Batuli who replied. "One who can afford to dress well does."

The girl herself added, "We're not hard up for household helpers in my place. If we had had to do household work we would have. But I haven't come here to have a mother-in-law boss me around."

"Just look at her spouting off. If you're here to perform worship, you can traipse on back to your room. Who asked you to come here anyway? You don't let others go about their business, but put on a big show."

The daughter-in-law felt irked. "I didn't come here to get in anybody's way. If I stay in my room, all I hear is grumbling that I lock myself up and don't show my face. What did I do to end up in this kind of house?"

Everyone present was enjoying the high drama. In the meantime Rupamati arrived and escorted her sister-in-law away. The mother-in-law's roar went on increasing. "You tell me, Dahalni Bajyai, if Kali-yuga has arrived now or not. Did you notice the country woman in her speaking? I didn't say a word; she was the one making a bluster. What wretchedness having to listen to such talk! I did complain to my husband."

With that she began to weep. The bride ought to have been from a respectable family, with no regard for affluence. Who was ever satisfied with a second party's wealth? Her husband hadn't listened to her but followed the advice of slippery tongues. Hadn't that Muse[63] Pyakurel strongly insisted? They had failed to preserve ancestral property, yet they were of good stock. Hadn't the prospective bride's grandfather received land worth ten thousand rupees as a gift on the occasion of a solar eclipse?[64] Hadn't she seen what it was like nowadays? How bright Ramu's fortunes had been! Thanks to the girl everything was just dandy, they said. Such a girl they had let get away, and ended up in the trap of awfulness personified. Kupre claimed people were saying that it was written in Ravilal's horoscope that his wife would bring him a fortune.

Dahalni Bajyai—"It's better not to have any daughter-in-law than to have such a sharp-tongued one. Why do you bow down to her? If my daughter-in-law talked to me that way, I'd hire a band and get my son another wife. That would be the end of the girl's pride."

Dhai Budhi—"Maybe it's in her fate to share her husband with a co-wife, what with her low-caste ways.

---

[63]A nickname (Moo-seh) applied to someone with a noticeable wart.
[64]In order to avert misfortune, donations are often made to Brahmins during eclipses.

It's disgusting! What times these are! In our days we never saw such women."

Madam Pandit—"Didn't you see the other day what a grand show they put on for the sixth-day ceremony of Ramu's son? Food galore and whatnot—dishes filled with sweets. They marched around eighteen plates of the stuff. Havilal said how very tasty the vegetables and *achar* were. You couldn't see any leaf-plates—everything was white dinnerware. Ramu is a real show-off."

Pathakni Nani[65]—"They say even the toothpicks were made of silver!"

Dahalni Bajyai—"Why not spend money swindled from the Terai in style? If they had earned it honestly. . . . They raked in money in their hick courthouse down there. And as soon as he got his job, he said he'd either make it big or fail for trying. And he was indeed lucky."

Madam Pandit—"Muse's daughter is plain lucky. What can we do! We can't get anything to go right since she entered the family. How could someone with two buck teeth have turned out good? She sent her father-in-law on his way within a year. How many more will she down? From what I see, Ravi's face has been gloomy ever since she set foot here."

Dahalni Bajyai—"There's every reason it should be, Bajyai! Your son is a full-blooded young man! As handsome as they come and fair-skinned. Baral's daughter doesn't measure up—even to his feet!"

It became unbearable for Batuli—hearing all the backbiting going on about her mistress. Having a wicked tongue, she spoke out. "Yes, how could she ever be a match? Your son is a great pandit, educated, who never comes back home before the cannon booms. There's not a day he doesn't make people wait two or three hours to serve him dinner. The poor fellow has no time even to breathe for all the work. And how can he come on time? He was kowtowing to Chete, Dhanamane, Babucha and Bhikhacha the other day. Isn't it so, Pathakni Nani? When

---

[65] "Nani" is a term of address applied to girls, or more generally a term of endearment for women younger than oneself. Pathakni Nani is the daughter of Banshi Pathak referred to above.

I escorted you, did you see him with them where they sing hymns?" (Pathak's daughter couldn't openly say yes; her face turned blue.) "How suavely he exhaled the smoke. What they said—disgusting! I forget everything so quickly. Oh, I remember now! 'Bam, Shivashankar!'[66] Madam's young son is good! Very good in fact! His look is always sombre, his eyes buried in his hands, his lips always dry, the brightness of his face gone. And then lots of income. His wife's money box is empty. Some days back, the lock was found broken."

She had gone overboard. Madam Pandit turned into a lioness upon hearing her son picked apart in front of everybody by a mere maidservant brought by her daughter-in-law from her parents' house. Batuli had rattled off everything in a single breath, with the force of a waterspout. Thus she couldn't interrupt her. She stood up suddenly, grabbed her hair and began to beat her mercilessly. "You damn whore! How dare you dishonour my son! How dare you badmouth him with things that aren't true! You fat sow! You were so thin when you came I could have blown you over. Now that you've fattened up on my food, you can afford to shoot off your mouth."

With these rabid words she slapped her cheek again and again. The girl for her part was not to be taken lightly. She was about to strike the old lady with a raised hand when Rupamati, having heard the commotion, came running and caught her in time. The girl made signs of being about to bite Rupamati, but two or there ladies grabbed hold of her and didn't allow her to move. She let out a cry. "Help! Help! The king to my rescue! They both want to kill me!"

By then, though, Rupamati had already disengaged her mother-in-law and taken her upstairs. Baral's daughter didn't have the courage to speak. The other women also condemned Batuli. Thirty or forty people gathered in the courtyard were asking, "What happened? What happened?" Ravilal arrived and sent them all away.

---

[66] An expression uttered to please the god Shiva, often by yogis while smoking hashish.

He knew quite well how to deal with such a situation. There was no one who didn't know him among the hooligans. There was every reason for them to dance to his tune. They could whoop it up with him and then cheat him. Ravilal heard the whole story after his arrival. His temper rose fiercely. His incensement over Batuli was allayed with two or three kicks to his wife. Baral's daughter yammered for a while, but Rupamati calmed her back down. It was a problem for poor Rupamati having so many to console.

Ravilal had drive and an imposing air, but in front of Batuli he was usually unable to bring forth a peep or look her in the face. Once she screwed up her eyes at him as if they were full of tears, he assumed the look of a person standing motionless with a dead cat clasped to his body; he had not the courage to speak. Women sitting there felt a chill in their hearts. They got the opportunity to digest their food. Their logical instincts told them that there was something amiss about Ravilal's behaviour. All eventually understood the reason, but no one saw fit to open their mouths.

Mr. Sharma arrived in the evening. He heard every detail bit by bit. The poor man, after a whole day of exhaustive labour, found no peace at home. The neighbours added their comments. "What's going on? Is the criminal court in session at your place?" He thought long and hard, but what could he do? If you scratch your body the dirt will show, it's said. He was all the more worried because his brother had failed to do anything about Batuli. It was out of the question to let Batuli stay, it hardly being wise to let the seeds of strife take root. If she were thrown out, whose honour would she attack, what embarrassments would she cause? It was like the saying, "If I speak out, my mother will die; if I don't, my father will eat dog's meat."

Distressed at heart, he rose to his feet. In the meantime a lawyer friend had come to see him. If he didn't share his troubles with a friend, who could he share them with? This was how to go about dampening the fires burning in his mind. It was decided that nobody should say anything. If she got pregnant, there would be problems, but even if she did it wasn't that there wouldn't be some way out, so there was nothing to worry about.

Drive her out on some pretext and if that didn't work and she made a hue and cry they'd get a man to come forward. If he accepted, that would be that. As luck would have it, Batuli's father arrived from Chepetar to deliver ghee, beaten rice and mustard seed husks used for making *achar* to her mistress. Madhuvan had told him, "My daughter must have adjusted by now, so you take your daughter back with you." And Mr. Sharma handed Batuli over to her father. Batuli for her part did not complain, thinking it might create problems for the Baral family if she made a fuss; she went home quietly. Rumours that Ravilal had maintained illicit relations with Batuli reached Chepetar even before Batuli did.

ಬಂಡ

Chapter 9

The mourning of Pandit Chavilal came to an end, and Mr. Sharma and his younger brother changed back into normal dress.[67] No one undergoes separation from parents without some disturbance to one's stars; there are no words to describe the mountain of grief that comes crashing down when parting provides the tumultuous occasion. A river of money flows, one's well-wishers are miffed over trifles, squabbles with others occur for no reason, trivial matters cause upset, unanticipated misfortune arrives. And so Mr. Sharma passed the year of mourning with great difficulty.

"Ravi, you've passed three courses; now finish one more. Why spoil things for nothing? You think it right to spend your life with street dogs? This time won't come back. Afterwards you'll be sweating blood." Mr. Sharma was fed up that no matter how much he talked sense to his younger brother it didn't sink in.

His brother was acquiring an even brighter name for himself among the hooligans. When the Phagu festival[68] came around he roamed the city, with his pockets filled with red powder and four-paisa shells of lac in each hand to hold it. At his side were Bire, Dale, Kusicha, Babucha, Sukucha and others. Their hands were not empty either. Mr. Sharma's brother bore all expenses. What it was was fun, pure and simple. No woman sitting in a window escaped. When four or five of them threw their shells in rapid-fire succession, at least somebody was bound to get hit. When the shells burst against pale cheeks, how red those cheeks then appeared! Mr. Sharma's brother would remark, "To make their faces red with shame, and then

---

[67]Mourning dress, worn for one year, consists of totally white attire.
[68]The festival of colours held in February-March celebrating Krishna's escapades with the cowherdesses.

on top of that to have the red powder land on them—they looked like nymphs!"

He would hang around with his gang and do some swaggering at the main hangout of his quarter. Who had it in her to escape untouched, free of red powder? On the day of the Shivaratri festival,[69] they followed tradition by staying up the whole night. Without Ravi the rowdies felt completely out of sorts. At his command many doors were unhinged and taken away. Mortars owned by Newars for pounding rice disappeared. There was no need to waste money on fruits and vegetables—they were growing in neighbourhood gardens. Everything was cooked over a bonfire at the main hangout.

Hemp was smoked to aid digestion. Ravi was not to be outdone in celebrating any festival. Ten or twelve rupees was nothing for him. By now he had a taste for gambling, and used to lose up to three or four hundred rupees. His brother didn't give him so much as a paisa, so where did the money come from? A cause of wonder among neighbourhood friends. But his buddies and relatives knew the secret. Nobody had the courage to say anything for fear he'd get angry.

The more Ravilal's lordship over the lanes increased, the more his wife's control over him hardened. Formerly money was kept in pockets; locks were not secured to boxes. Now something smelled wrong, and Rupamati, on orders from her husband, kept a stern watch over everything.

Nothing was lost. Ravi used to pry money out of his mother by repeated threats, which made her shed abundant tears, but now it was hardly likely that he could force money to rain down on him this way. Therefore, in order to get anywhere, he had to dance to his wife's tune—she whose money box was never empty. The reason was that, though Madhuvan Baral had obtained just a one-third share of the ancestral property, it was a tidy sum. His elder brother was somewhat of a dullard; not an ounce of cleverness to him.

---

[69]The festival celebrated in February-March in honour of Shiva.

Shushupal's economic condition was still not good by the time he was of marriageable age. He was in dire straits, as a matter of fact. Thus it was a trial to arrange a match for him. With great difficulty he was betrothed to Paneru's daughter in Bhanjyang, by taking out a *pathi*[70] loan. The sixty Mahendramalli coins[71] chinked down were not enough, so during the marriage he had to add three pairs of dresses, flowers, a necklace and a nose ring to get his way.

It was not as difficult to arrange a marriage for the second son, Madhuvan. For one thing he was quick-witted, and on top of that Shushupal had a daughter. Success was met with by promising to give this daughter in marriage with the new daughter-in-law's brother. (It was sometimes very useful to have a daughter!) They would have been at a loss what to do if no exchange could have taken place. The old man was well off by the time the youngest son got married. There was every reason for him to feel cheerful, having obtained, as he did, unexpected wealth from a childless relative. He held his son's marriage in undeniably grand fashion.

After he received his share of property, Madhuvan started raking in large sums by lending out his money on interest throughout the village. A home with three sons and one daughter was just fine. The daughter, being the only one, was the darling of her mother. The latter cried when she left to go to her husband's home to mourn her father-in-law's death. And why shouldn't she? For one thing, it is natural for women to have a special place in their hearts for their daughters. On top of that, Baralni Bajyai had delegated full responsibility for their property to her daughter, and the key of the treasure room dangled from her blouse.

Madhuvan for his part was a strange sort; as soon as he set foot out of the house, his wiles began. He used his debtors to plant rice in his fields. He went on increasing

---

[70] *pathi* = 4.546 l. This was a form of cash loan in which repayment was made in kind. Such a practice was, strictly speaking, unlawful during the Rana period.

[71] The first fifty-paisa coins minted in Nepal, during the reign of Mahendramalla (16th century).

the rate of interest on his loans to *savai*[72] or *pathi*, and summarily seized defaulters' houses and fields. If anyone came to pay back a loan, he'd quibble over every last paisa. The poor tenants dared not raise their voice; to do so was to invite attack by a tiger. His influence on the outside was consequently great. But as soon as he stepped inside the house, his presence of mind left him. When his wife told him to stand he stood; when she told him to sit he sat. He didn't utter a peep. People were always wondering what powers his wife possessed that she could make a mouse of him.

She didn't let a Brahmin be employed to cook rice, though sometimes she set her husband to the task, and this was how she performed her wifely duties. There was no time for odd jobs about the house. "I'm the one who collected all this property. It's all due to my good luck that we have so much to be proud of," she explained to all friends who came to visit her.

"The *karda* is sharper than the *khukuri*,[73] the son is wiser than his father" is the dharma of Kali-yuga. And so it was that Baral's daughter turned out smarter than her mother. Gradually the daughter's life-style became downright luxurious. Being an only daughter, she had been allowed to play the tyrant. It was difficult to control her. Madhuvan had it in his head that his daughter had got good training from looking after things, and this was the same reason his wife felt so bad about sending her away. It was their daughter who knew all the ins and outs of the household; everything had been in her hands.

The worry was how to run the house themselves, now that the new daughter-in-law was in her new home. (Why should the mother-in-law trust the bride, though?) Neither of her parents cared what their daughter might have taken away with her. After the mourning period for her father-in-law, she came to her parents' home once a

---

[72]One quarter. The maximum legal interest chargeable on loans during the Rana period was ten percent.

[73]The *khukuri* is the long curved sheathed knife used in everyday life. The *karda* is a smaller knife of the same shape carried in a sheath on the sheath of the larger one.

year, and whether she carried off this or that no one could say.

With so much wealth pouring in from her parents' home there was no reason for Ravilal not to let his wife call the shots. And there was no reason for her not to crow. The gnashing of teeth steadily increased at their home. How would the mother-in-law, who could not bear the sight of her Lakshmi–like elder daughter-in-law, ever come to an understanding with the shameless, lazy younger one? The latter's nature was indeed peculiar. She never emerged from her room till the sun rose, no matter how much others tried every trick to get her out earlier. Her sleep was imperturbable.

But she had a great wish to have a son. After taking a bath in the morning, she spent two or three hours reciting and performing worship. Every day she revered a Shiva lingam. Every Tuesday and Saturday she went to visit the Santaneshvar temple. People were astonished to see such religious devotion at such an early age.

Rupamati would have the morning meal ready by nine o'clock. There was not a single day her sister-in-law went to the kitchen in a good mood; she always arrived grumbling. As soon as she sat down to eat she began to complain about the grams and green vegetables. Sometimes she said, "Yuck! Who can eat grams boiled like this?" At other times she went back downstairs without eating, saying, "The vegetables you gave me are a fly head's worth. What did you think—that I'd pile up on rice?" She went to her room immediately after her postprandial washing of hands and mouth, and wouldn't come out of it the whole day. Delicacies were prepared there; sweet aromas were continually wafting out. Her cooing with Ravilal could be heard three floors up.

What every human should evince are kindness and respect for one's elders. When these are missing, then even those who win the Three Worlds or the Fourteen Realms[74] have no sense of shame.

---

[74]The Three Worlds are heaven, earth and hell. Heaven is further subdivided into six, and hell into seven realms, yielding a total of fourteen.

Now the mother-in-law dared not utter a peep; it was Baral's daughter's voice that was full-lunged. One day Mr. Sharma went to the kitchen to have his meal. There was no water in the jug, and in an offended tone he said to his mother, "What's wrong with this house? I don't understand it. There's no water in the jug when I sit down to eat, no water in the pot to wash up afterwards with. I'm fed up! Where has Chameli gone? She should bring water on time."

"You're right, it's been quite a while since she went to fetch water. She must be gossiping at the tap. There's no one to call her back." With that, the old lady began shouting from the window.

Chameli arrived. The old lady admonished her. "Does it take an hour to bring a jug of water? You've been fooling around with someone. My son has come for food. He's had to wait for water. This is totally uncalled for."

"What can I do? I don't have ten hands. I was on my way back with the water when your younger daughter-in-law sent me off to buy four paisas' worth of *sarsyu*.[75] I told her you needed water upstairs and to let me take the jug up, but she wouldn't listen. She told me to set it down and that she would take it up herself. What was I to do? I only have two hands."

Upon hearing Chameli's reply, the mother-in-law let out a roar to shake the whole house. Her yelling penetrated to the ground floor room. "You see, Havilal. How can I possibly calm down when outrages like this occur? Baral's mother (she meant her younger daughter-in-law) is bent on destroying our household! What good ever came out of relations with the lower sort? Only blind people should have anything to do with such a sorry excuse for a Brahmin's daughter. She stays in the room and issues commands. As for household work, she wouldn't move a twig from here to there. If she came from a good family things would be all right, but her ancestors probably wore dirty loincloths and herded buffaloes. How could their descendants have any sense! And how could so much unexpected inheritance have

---

[75] A variety of mustard. The seed is used as a spice.

come their way? I've nowhere seen a girl unload money the way she does. Easy come, easy go."

Baral's daughter could no longer bear to hear her mother-in-law's criticism of her father and grandfather. She went upstairs expatiating to herself. "I haven't touched so much as a broken cowrie of their property, and yet she talks about my ancestors that way! Hah! If her own ancestors had been anything, she'd have reason to speak. Whose great-grandfather was it who was driven off and had to go to Benares with a *kalpurush*[76] offering? Wasn't it said his face was blackened? The curse of the stars was sure to fall on someone: whose grandfather do they say had to walk the streets carrying a baby pig? Who are they to be taunting others? They're mad because I have money from my parents' home and enjoy life. I haven't spent a paisa of anyone else's money. If I spent money it's my father and grandfather's property I'm enjoying."

These burning words of Baral's daughter pierced the heart of her mother-in-law. Mr. Sharma for his part had no clear knowledge of his genealogy. He was shocked to hear such things. Rupamati turned blue. She could hardly imagine that a daughter-in-law would dishonour her mother-in-law that way. The old lady replied, "Just listen to this low-caste mouth! Always coming back at you. A true widow's daughter![77] What a curse to have to listen to her sound off! She's turned Ravi into a sheep."

"I have not! If you're dissatisfied, I'll leave. Just say the word, and I'll be back at my parents' home like that. I didn't come because we had nothing to eat," Baral's daughter ranted.

Mr. Sharma came down from the kitchen. "Disgusting! If you stir around in the sewer, you'll get splotched. Mother, why are you yelling?" With these words Mr.

---

[76] A luxurious offering made to a Brahmin by members of the ruling class on the eleventh day following death on condition that he leave the locality. The usually poor Brahmins who accepted such an offering were looked down upon.

[77] Part of a proverbial expression of contempt, which goes on to say that the daughter falls into a vat and is boiled to death.

Sharma tried to calm his mother down. But how could she be calm?

"Am I to be dishonoured today by some bumpkin's daughter? She must have worms in her mouth to come up with scurrilous talk like that."

The poor lady couldn't enjoy her food that day. She was downcast to the end of it. In the evening she noticed that her younger son was also annoyed with her. All through the night she continued to be restless, remembering her daughter-in-law's words. Sleep's enemy, thoughts, drove away the heavenly repose.

☼☯

Chapter 10

What wonder that Mr. Sharma's love for Rupamati was increasing day by day! The younger daughter-in-law never cooked, and Rupamati didn't feel right letting her aged mother-in-law do so. Mr. Sharma's heart melted at seeing Rupamati not have time to breathe for all her household work. Pity welled up in him when he saw her flag in having to keep food waiting for hours for his brother. A cook was engaged.

Now Rupamati had enough time to look after and serve her own husband. She served her husband unfailingly around the clock, from the time he got up in the morning till he went to bed at night. Early in the morning she brought tobacco. When Mr. Sharma set the hookah gurgling, toothpaste, a jug of water for the latrine and a clay pot of water for washing hands were made ready. She stood waiting with a towel. When he finished brushing his teeth and went to bathe, he found a dhoti, towel, soap and related toiletries all in proper order.

Getting up betimes, Rupamati prepared the articles necessary for worship. Nothing was missing. Everything in the room was waiting for Mr. Sharma as he stepped out for a walk in the early morning hour. His wife arrived to set his clothing straight. The cook brought tea in between. As soon as Mr. Sharma went out she went upstairs, and the cook started to boil rice. She herself set about cooking the vegetables. The curried vegetables and *achar*, once ready, were placed in the dining area. Mr. Sharma, it could be said, never had to eat bad food. And when he went downstairs after the meal, he found water to rinse his mouth and hands with, and a towel and a toothpick; and a small box filled with pan and betel nuts was also in the room. She dressed him in a well-brushed coat and well-brushed shoes.

Rupamati spent the whole day reading books and twisting wicks. Her mother-in-law was taken up with worshipping, while her own work was to prepare for worship and twist the wicks. Mr. Sharma had interested her in Hindi, and she had got to the point where she could understand novellas and short stories.

Dinner was ready for Mr. Sharma when be came back home in the evening. Even in the evening he never had to complain about not finding something in its proper place. All chores were performed without murmur; his wife never looked irritated. She was unable to talk without a smile—a smiling face and sweet words. There was no one who came to her home who was not happy to be with her. One might have thought that in caring for her husband day and night she did not pay attention to other household duties. But this was not so. Nothing escaped her attention; nothing was lost or wasted. Cobwebs were nowhere to be seen. Dirt and rubbish was non-existent. (She had no access to her sister-in-law's room, so nothing could be said about conditions there.) It was Mr. Sharma's great good fortune to have such a beautiful and modest jewel of a woman as his wife!

Rupamati felt terribly bad that her sister-in-law had uttered heated words to her mother-in-law, and had thus caused her pain. Mr. Sharma was also at a loss. He couldn't imagine how his sister-in-law could be so shameless as to express such unutterable sentiments so callously to his mother's face, slashing away at a heart that already had a skewer, as it were, in it. There was a long discussion between husband and wife in their room that same night.

Mr. Sharma—"Such women also come into this world, I see! Utterly shameless! How could she insult my mother in front of me?"

Rupamati—"I also felt terrible listening to her, and almost lost my senses once. How could she talk so vulgarly and spread such false stories? She should have some respect for a brother-in-law. But then, how could someone without any respect for her mother-in-law think highly of her brother-in-law?"

Mr. Sharma—"Ravi has got himself rolled up into a ragged mess! It's a shame for him to be a fly in the fist of such a woman."

Rupamati—"No, they say your brother's mother-in-law is very cunning—the kind that can make a flying bird fall. Maybe her daughter learnt the same things."

Mr. Sharma—"Come off it! what are you talking about, Rupa? You believe in such things? Ghosts, evil spirits, witches—that's all rubbish of the mind." Mr. Sharma let out a snicker.

Rupamati—"That's your nature: to laugh and take everything lightly. If I had that knowledge I'd have shown what it means to turn one's own husband into a sheep."

Mr. Sharma—"What need to learn that? You already know how to make people dance, Rupa! Look, I agree with you, so why learn your sister-in-law's magic? If she has things under her control, you have things under yours. She may utter spells to herself and get things done. But you work your magic, too, with those doe's eyes of yours, your upturned eyelashes and gentle smile with teeth gleaming like ivory, and that gentle voice like a cuckoo's. There's magic in your beauty; for her, it's all in her mind. You have power to charm by your ways; she, only by her wealth! You give heavenly bliss; she only gives worldly pleasure! That's the difference."

Rupamati—"Really, now! So much delirious talk in one breath. You really know how to say the pleasing word. Who can compete with you?"

Mr. Sharma—"Did I say anything that isn't true, Rupa? There are scores of women today burning with jealousy over your wealth of beauty."

Rupamati—"Let them die, get angry or do what they want. For me it's enough if I can please you."

Mr. Sharma—"To get back to the point: Our sister-in-law is going overboard; how can we carry on like this? No, I don't think it's going to be possible to stay together for long."

Rupamati—"Why did she end up as somebody who has seen and heard everything? She thinks nobody knows as much as she does. She's happy if everyone keeps quiet and lets her do whatever she wants. What kind of person is it that can't tolerate the least peep of criticism? On the morning of Tihar[78] she was taking a bath, rubbing her body with soap, and I just said, 'Is it right to be washing your hair early in the morning on a festival day?' She shouted at me. The other day on your birthday your cousin was talking to me before she left. She was telling me something, and then *she* arrived. She interrupted us and didn't let us continue. Your cousin told me before she left, 'Send someone to buy a book of etiquette for four paisa and let her digest it.'"

Mr. Sharma—"Never have dealings with the wicked! You're better off going hungry and tightening your belt. What can you get out of eating with such a person? How can Lakshmi live in a house where quarrels are always going on? It's hard to make ends meet no matter how much we earn. I'm fed up, Rupa! Shall we part ways with Ravi—what do you think?"

Rupamati—"Ram! Ram! What sort of talk is that? You'll court tragedy by separating from Babu. Even though his wife is pouring things in from her parents' home, for him it's a mere lick of the finger. It was a couple of days ago, wasn't it, that the Kabuli[79] was roaring at him in the morning? No sooner does money come into his hands than it goes up in smoke. How can he pay back loans? I heard he had four coats made with cashmere from the Marwari[80] Chattumal. He didn't pay for that either."

Mr. Sharma—"That's why I say we can't keep them with us. Who can put up with the roars of Kabulis and others day and night?"

Rupamati—"That's all the more reason not to send them away. It's for fear of you that they dare not claim the house and land now. Once we separate all the creditors will surround your brother, and then what?"

---

[78] The five-day festival of lights in October-November. The day referred to here is given over to the worship of Lakshmi, the goddess of wealth.
[79] Afghani businessmen used to come seasonally to Kathmandu.
[80] A business caste of Jains originally from Rajasthan.

Mr. Sharma—"How many loans can there be? To pay them back, we're not going to have to mortgage the property, are we?"

Rupamati—"Things don't look so good now. His bad habits aren't going to go away. His interest in gambling is increasing. How long will it take for him to finish off the house and land? It won't be nice to see your brother's condition then. Do you have the strength to see the brother born from the same mother as you—you spent years eating, playing and fighting with—without a rag to his name, with nothing to eat, roaming the alleys like a street dog?"

Mr. Sharma—"What do you want me to do—die? Nothing I've said has changed him. He's swimming in his wife's urine. If he keeps on going from bad to worse like this, how can he continue to stay in this house? Even when his wife scolded Mother it was Mother he got mad at."

Rupamati—"He hasn't grown up yet."

Mr. Sharma—"If he still has no sense at his age, I can't imagine he'll ever have any."

That day the conversation between husband and wife found no end. Mr. Sharma suddenly fell asleep during the talking. That same night Baral's daughter was putting things into Ravilal's ear.

Baral's daughter—"How many days am I supposed to go on tolerating the old lady's bellyaching? It's not one day—it's every day she grumbles, and for what? I haven't taken a paisa from anyone's father. She even goes after my long-gone grandfather and great-grandfather—the old windbag!"

Ravilal—"That's the way she is. When she gets angry she goes blind and loses all sense of what to say and what not to."

Baral's daughter—"If she has something she wants to say, let her say it to her favourite daughter-in-law. Does she ever utter a nasty word to her? As for us, we can do absolutely nothing. If she doesn't like me she can drive me out."

Ravilal—"Come off it! What are you talking about? Who has the courage to drive you out?"

Baral's daughter—"What do I have to fear even if they do? Even now do I depend upon them? And why should you hang around for nothing to massage your brother's feet? Is it proper to stay after such insults?"

Ravilal— "My brother has said nothing; how can I talk about separation? It would be hard for me to suddenly bring up the subject, let me tell you!"

Baral's daughter—"If a snake has no poison and a man no defiance, what's the use? It's my own unlucky fate. If it wasn't so, would I be suffering all these annoyances?"

With that Baral's daughter broke into a sob. The hour was late, and Ravilal was overtaken by sleep. The matter was left hanging.

From the next day, Ravilal's attitude gradually changed. He seemed on the verge of affronting his brother, he wouldn't agree with his mother for anything, and when he went to have food he would explode that his sister-in-law had insulted him by not giving him enough curry.

One day Chameli forgot to set out water for the after-meal ablutions, and for that small offence the poor girl received a slap and a kick. It had reached the point where she could no longer stay, but what was she to do? She told the wet-nurse that she could not get along with Ravilal and his wife, and so decided to leave the house she had grown up in, without telling anyone.

The younger daughter-in-law's outrages worsened day by day. She was so proud of her parents' home that she had stopped comparing it with any other. Her mother-in-law had been totally estranged from her since the day she had rankled her with bitter words; she didn't look her in the face. Seeing the woman deference to whom had kept her in check now bow, she began to go about with an expanded chest. And respect for her sister-in-law? Why, even though she might have shown respect to street dogs, she couldn't stand the sight of her. But Rupamati never replied discourteously to her, never uttered unseemly words. She knew toleration. She endured in silence whatever was said. That there was nothing greater than toleration was her firm belief. She had put up with her mother-in-law's rebukes day in and day out, and now both her mother-in-law and husband were fond of her. But Baral's daughter took a quite different view of her powers of toleration. She thought her sister-in-law a weak and useless coward, and insulted her as such. Mr. Sharma usually had little time to be at home, the burdens of his work keeping him busy day and night. Ravilal had become a puppet, dancing as he was made to dance. Chameli, a veteran servant, sometimes came close to being arrogant, but even she had left. Now who would dare to challenge Ravilal's wife?

If Chameli, who had been a part of the family—was on easy terms with everyone and knew what made them tick—could no longer bear things and had to slip away, how would a new servant ever survive?

Regarding the new one, Mr. Sharma said, "Nothing has been settled yet. While she was cleaning the floor, Ravilal's wife told her to go buy some *svari*s and *jilebi*s, and when she didn't, she exploded and called her a common whore, and the maid got up and left."

Whatever bad traits Madam Pandit may have had, she nevertheless cherished an abiding love for Chameli. She would jump on anyone who criticized her. She knew what a muddle things would be if her trusted servant left.

As time went on her limbs failed her, and given the constant verbal onslaught of Baral's daughter, she had stopped standing up for Chameli. It had all been too much for Chameli. How could things be right when she, who had for days been tending the old lady's bedpan, had to leave her to no purpose? Servants were changing every half month due to the sin incurred. Mr. Sharma would find a woman somewhere and set her to work, but how many days would a nominally paid labourer hold out? The load of housework that fell to Rupamati increased steadily. But she kept quiet. She never uttered a word, knowing that if she turned up the heat, her husband was ready to send his brother packing.

☎☏

Chapter 11

The Luintels, husband and wife, were sad to hear about the distress Rupamati was having to endure. Even though they could explain away the trials of a daughter-in-law as being natural, compassion waxed in them at all the kicks and other forms of pain inflicted upon her by her sister-in-law. Her mother began regularly to send Sante's sister to her with food. Rupamati never ate any of it without first dividing it up among all the family members. Baral's daughter, though, pushed her share away, saying that she was not one to eat food sent by other people's parents. Rupamati always set that share aside, there being servants who would eat it.

Thinking that, for all the household work, her daughter might be short of time, Rupamati's mother twisted bunches of wicks and sent them over. Once Rupamati's aged mother-in-law expressed the wish to offer a hundred thousand wicks to Lord Budhanilkhantha.[81] Upon hearing that, Luintelni Bajyai twisted wicks with the help of her close friends and sent them to her. Rupamati herself twisted some. Her mother-in-law's wish was fulfilled.

Luintelni Bajyai was greatly desirous to have her daughter visit them for two or three days. She sent for her many times, but nothing was heard from her. How strange! Other people's daughters would cry, shriek and send enquiries if someone didn't come to fetch them regularly back to their parents' home. What feigned anger they worked themselves up into! Upon hearing the voice of their parents' servant, they grabbed their sari and rushed downstairs immediately, and arrived home way ahead of their fellow wayfarer. If they could not go

---

[81] A famous image outside Kathmandu of the god Narayan sleeping on the serpent Shesh.

forthwith, having started work they had to finish, they would put their hand to the task with renewed zeal. It didn't take long to complete. Could they but have worked that way all the time, all the grumbling mouths in the house would have been silenced. If for some reason they couldn't go and the servant had to return without them, who could bear to witness their pointless rantings and ravings? It didn't matter how much housework remained to be done; if they could go home, they felt as if they had slain an eighteen-foot tiger.

Rupamati didn't have any particular longing to go home. It wasn't because her parents lived far away, for how long did it take to go to Dhobidhara from Kaldhara? It was only that she worried that if she went it would be a burden on her mother-in-law and husband, and the housework might suffer. Thus she refused to go. If Baral's daughter went to Chepetar, she came back only after two months. Rupamati never gave a thought to going home and enjoying herself, and thereby causing problems for everyone.

Luintelni Bajyai had another source of pain greater than this. She had no other offspring than her one daughter, and the latter showed no sign of soon having any of her own. It would be horrible to have all issue end on a daughter's side for lack of progeny. She was very concerned about what to do. Her fasting and performing of rituals increased dramatically. She took nothing but fruit on the eleventh lunar day throughout the year.[82] She fasted on Tuesdays in honour of Ganesh, worshipped Bhagavati on the eighth lunar day, and performed the rituals for Lord Shiva on the thirteenth. She paid regular visits to Vajrayogini and Dakshinkali. She promised to make a grand offering to Karyavinayak if her wish was fulfilled. On Saturdays she went to Shobhabhagavati.[83] Quite often donations were distributed at home too.

---

[82] The eleventh day of the waxing and waning lunar month is traditionally one of abstaining, particularly from meat.

[83] Vajrayogini, Dakshinkali and Shobhabhagavati are all significant temples to the Mother Goddess (Bhagavati) in one of her various forms. Karyavinayak is the name of a temple to the elephant-faced god Ganesh in the southern part of the Kathmandu Valley.

Luintel Baje for his part served holy men and spiritual practitioners. This was the dream they dreamt day and night. Nevertheless, their wish had not yet come true.

Rupamati also had the same worry. Was there any reading a man's mind? Would her husband, considering that she had borne him no issue, take a co-wife? She did please her husband—extremely so—so there was not much to fear on that account. Still, the word "co-wife" sounds a knell in the heart of every woman. There was indeed reason for her thoughts to turn that way. Old traditional-minded women had already raised the question with her mother-in-law, saying that another marriage was necessary to ensure offspring. Nobody dared to talk about such things to Mr. Sharma. But why should anyone keep from doing so with her mother-in-law?

One day Mr. Sharma consulted a doctor friend of his about Rupamati. The difficulties of having a child from an early marriage were discussed. But Rupamati heard nothing about this.

It was Madam Pandit's cherished dream to set eyes on a grandchild in her old age. She regularly worshipped Satyanarayan in hopes of a grandson or granddaughter. She would share her anxieties with her old female friends. Rupamati had been married long. It was not a good sign for her. To keep a house going there needed to be offspring. What use was it to have good character and youthful beauty without any? There was no use. Talk began to occur regularly to the effect that it would be best to find a new match.

Who does not fall to wondering, knowing the nature of women? When husbands bring home a co-wife, some wives do not protest by crying, shrieking or otherwise exercising their throats. Instead they are quick to recommend co-wives for others' daughters, and seeing others discomfited, they clap, laugh and talk their heads off before they finally settle down.

There was no dearth of people to pronounce blessings on Rupamati for her future good fortune and attainments. Luintel Baje's piety bloomed, Madam Pandit's stars brightened. Luintel Baje performed spiritual exercises every day at twilight on the banks of the river Bagmati. He spent his evening hours serving holy men.

It was the day of Shivaratri. The lordly sun was sinking, setting the western sky ablaze. The whole range of mountains covered with snow and lit by the sun's rays were utterly resplendent. Devotees of nature were filled with supreme joy to see such magnificence. The glitter of the solar light in the unsullied waters of the Bagmati—a passing remembrance of the day—was the signal to Luintel Baje that the time had come to do his evening exercises, and imparted a feeling of pure joy. Evening gradually approached with its spread wings. Luintel Baje sat down, crossing his legs. He had just gotten up after completing his exercises when he had a vision of a divine form, his eyes falling on a holy man who had come to stand in the presence of Lord Pashupatinath. Luintel Baje followed after him. The man, having reached Mrigasthali,[84] abruptly turned around and asked, "What do you want, my son? Why are you behind me?"

Upon hearing these words, Luintel Baje folded his hands and made a request in Hindi, "My lord, I am very agitated at not having offspring. I have become old; grant my daughter a son. This is my prayer."

"You are devoted to God. Very well, my son, go. It will be so." What soothing words! Luintel Baje could hardly control himself. Today his wish had been fulfilled; he had received a boon from a holy man. He closed his eyes and went on, giving thanks to God. After ten steps he looked around, but the sadhu had disappeared. He asked here and there, giving a description, but no one said they had seen him. He ran back and forth but did not find him. "What a fool I am! It didn't once occur to me to touch his feet! Now when will I get to see such a serene, powerful face again?" Luintel Baje spoke these words with a feeling of regret. But as he himself was a man of wisdom, his delusional state did not last long. The pandit headed on toward Guheshvari.[85]

---

[84] A forested area opposite Pashupatinath temple where Shiva once hid himself in the form of a deer.

[85] A temple of the Mother Goddess in the Pashupati complex.

Mohan Prasad Luintel experienced a peculiar feeling on that day. His mind was unclouded, so that everything seemed bright. After witnessing the circumambulatory ritual of Pashupatinath he set off for home. Today he felt a new surge of strength; as he walked along, his aged limbs did the work of a youth's. He reached home.

Luintelni Bajyai was waiting for her husband with fruit dishes, and by chance, as it was Shivaratri, Rupamati also had some leisure time. Madam Pandit was fasting. Rupamati, having set out fruits for the others, had gone to pay respects to Lord Pashupati. On her way back she thought of visiting her mother for five minutes, and she had just entered when her father arrived. It had been many days since the parents had met their daughter. Upon seeing her, her father blessed her with a downpour of flowers brought from the temple, and then told of all the events of the day. Tears flowed from Luintelni Bajyai's eyes; she was filled with happiness. For a moment she couldn't say a word. Rupamati blushed. It was but natural for a good person like her to feel shame. Luintelni Bajyai began to invoke various gods and goddesses out loud. To all she prayed, "Make the holy man's words come true." Rupamati, who had come for five minutes, didn't notice that half an hour had gone by. When the clock struck eight she became aware of the time. She set off immediately, saying it was late.

Fortunately her husband had not returned home; her service to him suffered no loss. All these things made her happy. During the night she had a strange dream, for to dream that the sun was frolicking in her lap was a wondrous dream indeed.

ஐᏣ

Chapter 12

Spring came. The cold-stricken poor and old began to stretch their limbs. Trees enervated by the battering of frosts were producing sap, their buds coming out everywhere, and their leaves getting to look green and glossy. Fruit trees were sprouting all over, producing fine scents. The singing of birds reverberated sweetly throughout the forest, bees hummingly sucked nectar from flowers, and gently blowing breezes rendered throngs of fair hearts blissful. Cuckoos, singing "Ko ho? Ko ho?,"[86] plunged headlong into the joy of spring. Only in the hearts of the bereft did fires of anxiety flame, at the memory of their loved ones. For them, even the cool rays of the full moon were ablaze. In all other respects spring, the season that saw a new year celebrated,[87] was universally looked upon as a pleasant time. Everyone seemed happy.

Mr. Sharma's mother had no peace of mind even during this delightful season. She passed restless nights. Her appetite decreased. She wanted to spend time in worship and prayer, but all sorts of things were playing havoc with her stomach. Suddenly, for no apparent reason, she lost herself to the world. But then she regained control of herself and turned her mind to worship. At times, she was further depressed at not being able to set eyes on a grandchild from Rupamati; at other times she worried about how her younger son would look after his wife and children. The thought of what fix her hellcat of a daughter-in-law, with no education to her name, might get them into made her head spin.

---

[86]The onomatopoetic rendering in Nepali of a cuckoo's song means literally "Who is it?"

[87]The official New Year's Day is celebrated in Nepal in the middle of April.

She was amazed upon occasion to see how the whole house functioned. The poor lady had no peace from any quarter. If Mr. Sharma had had no income and Rupamati no character, and she had had to depend on her younger son's earnings, and obey her younger daughter-in-law to boot, how distressing that would have been for her! Having to slink about in a hangdog manner within the same house where she used to lay down the law would have been more than painful. The wife of the son who supported the family worshipped her, praiseworthily enough, like a goddess, whereas the wife of the younger son, who had not a chipped paisa to his name, created unbearable torment. Was it any wonder she felt like one of the living dead?

Dahalni Bajyai, the wet-nurse and Kaptanni Bajyai sometimes got together, and by talking with them the old lady would calm down. One day the whole group gathered when the younger daughter-in-law had gone to her parents'; it was an opportunity to go to work on Madam Pandit's "shame." A long discussion began.

Dahalni Bajyai—"How can she cook all alone in her room? What kind of mentality is that? It would be okay if it was a family all crowded together in a hut, say, where it wasn't possible to provide good food for all. But with pride of wealth she has no taste for ordinary dishes. Here you're just three persons to yourselves, including your elder daughter-in-law. How can she go on preferring food in her room, and the two go on eating by themselves, and not sharing with all family members? What kind of style is that? Disgusting!"

Kaptanni Bajyai—"How could what the Puranas say be false? Have you forgotten the story told by Chalise Baje at Indrachowk during Chaturmas? If such persons weren't born how could Kali-yuga go on?"

Dhai Budhi—"It doesn't matter whether others call you great or not. You are what you are in your own eyes. If everyone calls you 'My dear sir' or 'My dear madam,' it goes to your head. Pathakni Nani is so clever. She's always getting people to plunk down money by praising them to high heaven. If you turn our friend's head, she wouldn't notice even if you cut a slice of flesh off her.

Break in while she's talking, and you won't live to tell about it. What an arrogant nature! How can the nature of a low-class creature ever be good—someone proud of inherited property?"

Dahalni Bajyai—"Her younger brothers and their wives are still young. She keeps her mother happy, so she has unlimited access to the coffer and can dip into it anytime she wants. She's keeping her husband going nicely, and has got him trapped like a fly in her fist. Let something happen to her mother's health, though, and then see how high she holds her head. Now she doesn't need anyone; doesn't treat anyone as human."

Kaptanni Bajyai—"How could a person who treats her brother-in-law and mother-in-law so cavalierly care about anyone else? Our coming to visit Madam Pandit doesn't please her at all."

Madam Pandit—"Heavens, the time to discuss my affairs is long gone! After going through the hardship of setting up a household and now having to witness these affronts—my heart cries! What am I to do? If I say, 'You're being highhanded,' she calls me a vulture. If I say nothing, I lapse into insensibility. I have no desire to stay in this house a moment longer."

Dhai Budhi—"My God, Madam! Can you be talking this way? Everything is going along well because you're around. The hour you leave, the ship will go down!"

Dahalni Bajyai—"Your younger daughter-in-law is riding roughshod over your poor elder one, and your younger son is also heading downhill. Bagvir told me he put up his sister-in-law's *tilahari* as collateral at the loan office."

Madam Pandit—"Enough! Don't let talk of him pass your lips, Bajyai! As soon as I hear his name, I start to smoulder. Once he gets his hands on something, it's as good as gone. He did what shouldn't be done by falling for his wife's seductions. If he had stuck to the right path, would he be in the mess he's in today? Would my daughter-in-law have been able to ride him like a horse? Now I can say nothing to his darling. If I do he shouts abuses at me; jumps all over me."

Kaptanni Bajyai—"Now she can afford to dance on someone else's head, so why not put on a show? If the full responsibility of running the household fell on her, she would see the sorry state she's in. It would be better to send them away."

Dhai Budhi—"Yes, how can you go on putting up with them after such exorbitant behaviour? It would be better if you say, 'Okay, take your share and go.'"

Madam Pandit—"What are you talking about? Whatever pain I have to bear from his ways, he is my son, after all. How could I accept that? If he doesn't come home one day I wonder where he's gone, why he hasn't come, what he's had to eat. Oh, my poor boy! Did he go to bed hungry, or did something happen to him? All these endless worries come over me. When I see his face, my love comes back; when I see him behaving the way he does it's my anger that surfaces."

Dahalni Bajyai—"What can you accomplish with your one-sided love? The one you love as a son—that son has turned out to be your enemy. What an age! Didn't you hear that the youngest Tivari boy kicked his mother down the stairs? Such people are also born."

Kaptanni Bajyai (covering her ears)—"Ram! Ram! What sort of news is this to have to listen to? I wonder which hell such immoral demons will enjoy. It's a sin just to hear about them."

Dhai Budhi—"There are many who keep their own parents from having a square meal. Such human beasts aren't sons but cadavers. Who do you think become worms in hell? Just such sinners."

Madam Pandit—"My elder daughter-in-law won't agree to parting with my son either. If we sent them off without dividing up the property, they'd slam us with a court case. He's already come of age. They say such petitions would be accepted by the court. If we split the property, in two days it would go up in smoke. He'd be walking around in sackcloth a beggar—totally cut off from us. How could I bear to see that?"

Dahalni Bajyai—"There's your daughter-in-law's home, come what may. That's why she's so proud. Why should she let things reach that state?"

Kaptanni Bajyai—"Can he live forever off his wife's money? It's only as long as her mother lives, isn't it? Let her sisters-in-law's time come, then she'll realize."

This kind of talk was going on when Mr. Sharma arrived. It did not proceed any further. At the time Mr. Sharma was in a constantly fine mood. Peace reigned at home. There was no quarrelling ever since the younger daughter-in-law had gone to her parents' home. He regularly received kudos from his bosses for the work he did. Some people, seeing his work, were green with jealousy on account of him. They had not the skill to do a job by applying their knowledge and exerting themselves; they longed for a good name on the basis of swagger. In the end, though, milk is milk, and water, water; the truth will out, come what may.

These envious souls whispered into the bosses' ears about how Mr. Sharma was an old crock with not three cowries' worth of sense to him. Thus one or two years had been a trying time for the poor man. On many an occasion he had become frustrated and lost all hope, having worked his hands and feet off—worked himself to death—without receiving any recognition. How many reports he had racked his brain over, working without thought of meals and sleep, and still the bosses would come up with something wrong. The wretched fellow was fed up. But one notion sustained him: the result of good work is good; in the end virtue wins out, and one's labours are never wasted. In this way he consoled himself. In his heart of hearts, he was content to find the things that had sprouted from his brain being implemented in office management, even though he received no nod of appreciation from the top.

To chafe at not obtaining official recognition for work well done is natural. Even so, he was not one to take pleasure in badmouthing his bosses in a fit of anger. It was something he repeated over and over to himself: that his office should not come under fire, or his bosses under a shadow of accusation. In the end his enemies could do him no harm. On the contrary, if he had wished harm on others, he would likely have achieved his ends. His prestige in the office gradually rose. His bosses were increasingly pleased with him; his ill-wishers' mouths fell silent.

 Mr. Sharma had no particular problems at home either. His wife left nothing undone to make him happy. Given her never-ending labours, he never had to say there was something that hadn't been done. Even before he stepped in the house Rupamati was showering love on him with a gentle smile and tender sidelong glances. The whole day's tedium lightened. She brought him tasty dishes on clean plates. She stood by with water for him to wash his hands and a towel to wipe them with—good service if ever there was. Mr. Sharma was in seventh heaven. His wife asked him about things she couldn't understand in the Hindi books. Sometimes she chatted with him. He took pleasure in hearing of the exceptional ways of women.

 Mr. Sharma was stuck with a younger brother who dealt him an occasional blow. Ravilal was indecent and uncontrollable. Mr. Sharma was irked at his inability to reform him. At the time Baral's daughter was at her parents' home, so he couldn't stir up trouble. If Mr. Sharma had been able to live as peacefully all the time, how well his food would have sat with him! And how greatly his vigour and energy would have increased!

 Mr. Sharma's life went on this vein. After one or two months women started whispering. Some began to tease him. His old mother's face took on a smile. There was a singular power women possessed. Close friends maintained records of pregnancies on a house-to-house basis, with the adeptness women have of keeping tabs on new-born babies. The news of Rupamati's pregnancy spread to all corners. The one thing her enemies had to console themselves with now vanished. And how happy her parents were to hear the news can scarcely be imagined. Baral's daughter, too, had come back from her home and heard the good tidings about her sister-in-law. Her face turned red in astonishment, and the only thing missing was tears.

☼☫

Chapter 13

There was not a single day during which Madam Pandit's sister-in-law[88]—and some sister-in-law she was!—wasn't engaged in research on other people's affairs. She felt uneasy if she lacked information on neighbouring households. Others' work may have come to a standstill, but she would not leave once talk got going. And her luck was such that there was no local shortage of house-to-house visitors. This younger sister-in-law was in the kitchen, her elder sister-in-law having sent her cucumber *achar*. The servant's daughter had come to deliver them. She began to chat with her.

Sister-in-law—"Well, well! Where has this lady come from? Your mother has totally forgotten me! I told her to come once. It's as if it was a sin for her to step into my home!"

Servant's daughter—"Oh no, Madam, my mother doesn't even have time to breathe. Her hands aren't free for a second. What's she to do?"

Sister-in-law—"My sister-in-law's luck is unheard of. How has she managed to keep your mother for any length of time? I heard the old woman has cheap rice and *gundruk*[89] soup put under her nose. If she eats, she eats; if not, so much the better. In our case, we provide the same food we eat, yet there's always an uproar. If the curry runs out it has to be prepared again; otherwise my husband gets angry. In order to keep my servant in such a fine way, I'm forced to scrub dishes myself four times a month. How much is your mother's monthly salary?"

Servant's daughter— "One rupee, Madam!"

Sister-in-law—"Ram! Ram! If they make her grind her old bones, they ought to show some consideration for her.

---

[88] The wife of her deceased husband's younger brother.
[89] Mustard greens that have been pounded, packed tightly in a clay pot, set out in the sun to ferment, and then dried.

How cruel! It's no use to talk about my sister-in-law. What's she doing these days?"

Servant's daughter—"The same worship."

Sister-in-law—"Who does the cooking?"

Servant's daughter—"Today Mr. Sharma got permission, so he went to the palace. His wife is in the kitchen by herself."

Sister-in-law—"What kinds of curry has she prepared?"

Servant's daughter—"One dish of potato and bamboo shoot, and one dish of *jhinjhari*."[90]

Sister-in-law—"Do they prepare *achar* or not?"

Servant's daughter—"Today it's cucumber *achar*. There's always an *achar*."

Sister-in-law—"How much oil or ghee do they put in? As much as we do?"

Servant's daughter—"Really, Madam, I can't say."

Sister-in-law—"How about Ravilal?"

Servant's daughter—"He's the same. I can't think of anything special."

Sister-in-law—"And his wife?"

Servant's daughter—"These days her dandruff is up. There's not a day she doesn't lash out at Madam Pandit."

The old woman was caught up in the talk and completely forgot to stir the curry. Her neglect came home to her when the vegetables were already smouldering. When she checked them, they were burnt. She blushed, and bid good-bye to Mr. Sharma's servant.

A big gathering of house-to-house visitors was held at her place that same day.

Khutte Aryal's younger sister, Pandit Buche's daughter, Guithe's wife's younger sister, Gajadhumme's wife's elder sister and Chande's grandmother congregated. Once they started their confabulating, they failed to notice the sun set. No house was spared their criticism; no one had the power to challenge them. They always let themselves go, and there was only one person, Rasbihari, who could beat them at their own game, with talk that

---

[90] Balsam apple, a creeper (usually known as *barela*) that produces a fruit used in making curry.

confounded heaven and earth. They were intimidated by him, but otherwise no one else had it in him to speak in their presence. All understood that that was the way they were.

Buche's daughter—"Have you heard, Madam? Someone was sent from Khardar Pande to Sitaula Baje to ask for his daughter. He was mad such clods were after her. He thought some high-class people would come asking. That's what they've been keeping their daughter for. Drew him up by the arm, he did. The man who came with the proposal ran way, they say."

Gajadhumme's sister-in-law—"What kind of character is that for Sitaula Baje to have? The poor girls—they could have been mothers of three or four children by now. How they must be aching!"

Buche's daughter—"They'll end up with troubles a black dog never had! What good can come of raising daughters the way they've been?"

Guithe's sister-in-law—"Proposals have come from so many places. The old man always reacts as if he could eat you whole! It's safe to say bridegrooms can be found for girls up to fourteen or fifteen. Now the eldest one is seventeen. My younger daughter was born on Bhai Tika;[91] she was born on Dasain Tika.[92] Who's going to step forward in the Brahmin community to put vermilion[93] on the girls now that they've become so old?"

Khutte's sister—"How beautiful is the elder one? Maybe it's true what they say: 'Good looks don't mean good luck.'"

Sister-in-law—"That's rubbish! My sister-in-law's daughter-in-law is beautiful, and her luck couldn't be better."

Chande's grandmother—"It's only a way to cheer up those without a beautiful wife. It takes luck to be beautiful."

---

[91] The last day of Tihar, on which sisters put a *tika* mark on their brothers' forehead.

[92] The tenth day of the Dasain festival, when *tika*s begin to be given to relatives.

[93] One of the acts the bridegroom performs during the wedding ceremony.

Khutte's sister—"You call your sister-in-law's elder daughter-in-law lucky? Madam, her sister-in-law has her on the skewer day and night almost."

Buche's daughter—"There's something wrong with her brain! What would be the harm for her in driving her brother- and sister-in-law out of the house? What would that back country daughter have to live off of? She'd just shrink down to nothing. If I were her I would grab her by the hair and throw her down the steps."

Chande's grandmother—"Her husband told her to do that but she didn't want to hear of separation. She said she couldn't see her brother-in-law suffer."

Sister-in-law—"That's all a facade! How did she manage to bring her husband around—the wily thing?"

Buche's daughter—"That was before they had any children. See what happens now they have a son. All hell could break loose over children."

Khutte's sister—"They say the younger daughter-in-law doesn't let her mother-in-law utter a word. The only thing she hasn't done is beat her!"

Gajadhumme's sister-in-law—"Old Madam Pandit has got a taste of things. How could she not pay for the sin of not tolerating her elder daughter-in-law and making her shed tears of blood day and night? *She* ought to beat her."

Sister-in-law—"And it was she who spoilt her son. She's tasting the fruits of having covered over her son's misdeeds in his childhood."

Chande's grandmother—"You can say that again! One day he emptied the pandit's pocket and went gambling. He was found out, and when his father gave him a few slaps, your sister-in-law wouldn't stand for it. How can children thrive under such conditions?"

Buche's daughter— "No one was allowed to touch her son; she'd come at you like a tiger. When I told her that her son had stolen cauliflower from Lalcha's garden, she'd play him up in his own presence: 'My son do such a thing! The poor boy doesn't know what it means to be greedy.'"

Khutte's sister—"Yes, it's a very bad habit your sister-in-law has. My son also once got a slap from her. He saw

Ravilal engaging in some illicit gambling, and went to tell her. She came back at him: 'When has he ever done such a thing? Why is it everyone hates my young boy? Why these false accusations?'"

Buche's daughter—"Did they gamble with *lalkhas*[94] or buttons? That's the way these city children become corrupt. She kept quiet back then under the delusion that it was all innocent recreation. They began to gamble with money thinking it was *lalkha*s and buttons. They started out small- and ended up big-time gamblers. She thought if people pointed out bad things, they'd turn him bad."

Chande's grandmother—"That's how your sister-in-law got her younger son into the mess he's in."

Gajadhumme's sister-in-law—"Nonsense! Who would wish evil and destruction on their own son or daughter?"

Khutte's sister—"Is it necessary to speak words? The way could be paved by deeds. Many women have brought their children down by not understanding this."

Such a conversation was going on. Pandit Rasbihari arrived—a very fun-loving sort. He knew how to fuel the women's talk by agreeing to everything they said. He was also a past master at cutting things short and turning the conversation around.

With women he never retreated. Everyone hushed the moment he entered. The pandit began his discourse—"Why, I wonder, has God created these women? With them it's all yakety-yak, a burden on their husband's back, a lack of wisdom, hack it up and feed them, a knack for laziness, a sack of betrayal in times of need, a tacky temper. What's the use? A monkey's tail is neither a stick nor a weapon. That's why I get so mad when women open their mouths."

Khutte's sister—"If there were no women, how could anyone create this world and keep it running? The same man born from a woman's womb will turn around and bear down on her."

Rasbihari—"That's what I said: if women stopped having wombs and everyone was born by themselves, just

---

[94]Pieces of used bangles that have been melted down.

think how much agony we'd be relieved of. Is the pain of a child in a womb anything to laugh at?"

While the pandit was still finetuning his speech, the master of the house arrived. Fear overtook the former towards what must have been going through the latter's mind at finding him amidst the women. It was true that his was a peculiar nature. He went to wherever women were gathered and pruned away at his erudition. He had not a paisa of income. Sometimes he chiselled, and at other times took a loan on interest. That was how he passed his life.

༄༅

Chapter 14

Baral's daughter's faith in the powers on high had been gradually declining. There was no sign of any offspring after even hours of worshipping Shiva every day. Now her sister-in-law's delivery date was near at hand; how could she find peace of mind? She began to flare up at even the smallest things. She would pick a fight on any pretext. The skin of a banana eaten by her mother-in-law, who was on a fruit diet, fell on the stairs. The younger daughter-in-law, whose habit it was always to descend quickly, like drum patter, slipped and all of a sudden lay sprawled out with a sprained back. She began to curse from the lower floor. "The old woman doesn't want to go herself but will send others on their way, by God! She's now to where she's putting banana peels on the stairs to slick them up. If her thoughts weren't on murder, she could have stuffed herself and thrown them out the window. How can I go on when it's hard just protecting my own body? When she can't take it she pretends to do ritual. Looking at her from the outside, can she be a real devotee? How clever she is at impressing those who don't know her real nature that she's a pious lady! I'd make a fool of myself now if I said she tried to kill me. I'd have to hear people questioning how a lady who devoted herself day and night to worship could do such a thing. Here I lie like this. Death comes to all, so why not to that old witch?"

Madam Pandit, having been charged with attempted murder, reached her limits of tolerance. To have remained silent would have been to accept the charge. There was no way not to speak out. "Control your tongue when you speak. How dare you say whatever you like just because you can open your mouth! When I threw the banana peels out, by chance one happened to land on the stairs. You understand? Even God fears the wicked. I said to myself, Nobody will give her any lip; and I can't stand sitting quietly by and letting you prattle away. How can you say such unthinkable things? It's not I didn't tell my husband." (Tears welled.) "It was written in my fate I'd have to tolerate such, and he for some reason agreed. What sin I must have committed in my previous life! Now I have to constantly hear such awful things! Curse my fate!"

Ravilal was down in his room. His wife's leg was hurt. He wondered if iodine should be applied. His wife replied full-throatedly. "What are you talking about—apply iodine! Is a little iodine going to heal this? This swelling will go down, but if my head was cracked what would you have done? How can you keep silent, knowing what your mother was intending? By now the wound is reaching my liver; it won't heal normally."

What could Ravilal say? If he agreed with what his wife said he would have to label his mother a murderess at heart. He looked on baffled, saying nothing. Unable to influence her husband's thoughts, Baral's daughter lost courage and began to execrate herself. "This has been my fate ever since I set foot in this house. I've never had a day of peace. I've had enough of sitting glum and saying nothing. I'm fed up to my neck. You, my fine hubby, are a radish from the same plot! The son of your mother, aren't you? Even today, when my life is at stake, you haven't said a word and just look goggle-eyed, so what hope do I have now? My hard service to you has all been for nothing. Haven't you heard that my cousin's husband let go at his mother's face? The old lady called my cousin a butcher. Then a big free-for-all broke out. 'You think you can make an outcaste of me by calling my wife a butcher,' is what her husband said to his mother, and then he took a swipe at her. The old lady had the living daylights scared out of her. From that day on she stopped uttering malicious words. Our old woman is considered respectable even when she commits high crimes. If I had been given in marriage to the son of Subba[95] Kirimiri, when he insisted so strongly, would I have to be going through all this hell? There's no trusting these money dealers. They can get a thousand rupees in one day by

---

[95]A high civil service post during the Rana period.

shady dealings. The next day Kumarichowk[96] can apply the screws and raid their property, and they become bankrupt. Kirimiri would be unable to buy land. He has Indrachowk and Asan[97] in his pocket. If our priest's wormy mouth hadn't blocked the way by making insinuations about the son of such a man, I wouldn't be in the horrible situation I am now. These days who can bear to see Kirimiri's extravagance?" Having said all of which, she began to shed bitter tears.

It would have been difficult for Ravilal to make it through a single day without taking sides with his wife. His nature was, now as before, to squander whatever he got his hands on. He didn't feel right not to say something. "Am I supposed to tell you that my mother intentionally tried to kill you? How can I say you're a thorn in my mother's side and she threw the banana skin on the staircase to kill you?"

Hearing this, Baral's daughter began to wail and moan the louder. Drawing out her speech and making facial contortions, she let her feelings be known. "So I'm useless, I'm no good, and your mother is simple and innocent—no sin in her heart? Good God! How could such a truth-loving woman do such a thing?" (She wiped away tears.) "I didn't care about my brothers. I went to my mother with tears in my eyes and kept bringing you money so you could live in style, and now this is the result. I'm beginning to taste the fruits of renouncing everything to call you husband and live 'under your protection.' Today I end up lumped up on the floor, and am taken for a fool to boot. What justice is that?"

Hearing such words from his wife, Ravilal felt his heart sink. Without any comment he jumped to his feet and strode off.

Baral's daughter spent one and a half days without a meal. Ravilal went to his mother, hoping that she would go to his wife and have it out with her and bring her back to the kitchen. One apology would set things right, but he broached the subject only to receive a barrage of words in

---

[96]The government auditing office during the Rana period.
[97]The central market areas in downtown Kathmandu.

response. "It's not my stomach that's hungry. If she wants to eat, let her; if not, not. What do I care about someone who's a witch doctor or a witch? She's always talking nonsense and creating a hullabaloo. A pumpkin won't fit in the mouth of a goat. This is the result of saying 'Yes, yes' no matter what she says!"

When Ravilal had gone to his wife to smooth things out, he had already received a royal reproof, so he was full of anxiety about how to bring her around.

His sister-in-law saw him and asked. "Babu, why so solemn? You should explain things to your brother! I tried my best, but it didn't work. What stubbornness is this from your wife?"

It was difficult for Ravilal to request his brother to try to make his wife take food. Through it all Baral's daughter remained unmoved by all blandishment. She was charged with electricity. Why should she go hungry out of anger with her mother-in-law and sob herself dry? She crammed her mouth with *pedas*[98] on the sly. She made Ravilal grimace by giving the impression of not even taking water. Who can understand women's exorbitances?

Rupamati didn't feel right not telling her husband about everything. But why should the stir her sister-in-law had created reach his ears? In the first place, he perhaps had innumerable problems of his own. On top of that, he had to manage domestic affairs. In the end, why should he be caused useless anxiety and concern by what she had to say? Thinking that no matter what was going on in the house he should be left in peace, she had up to now not broached the subject with him.

The conduct of an understanding woman is beyond compare. She knows that it's not good to tell her husband about one so-and-so doing such-and-such and another so-and-so quarrelling about this and that just after he comes back exhausted from a day at the office, instead of showing him the respect he deserves; or to act frivolously when he sits down to read. Rupamati had formed the conviction that it was not good for women to distress or

---

[98] A kind of sweet made of thickened milk.

alarm their husbands or to create misunderstandings between brother and brother or mother and son, and that if they refrained from doing so the world would be heaven. Thus she had kept silent. Now she could not help raising the matter. She thought it not good to keep her sister-in-law without food and give reason for malicious neighbours to clap their hands in delight.

Mr. Sharma heard everything through. He was distressed to no end to learn that such a mean accusation had been levelled against his mother. For a moment his vision blurred, and he said that it was a sin even to look upon the face of such a low woman. Rupamati was in an uneasy position. How could she control the situation? She raised the topic of her brother-in-law. "Ravilal is feeling low."

Mr. Sharma didn't care to hear her out and replied in no uncertain terms. "He's favoured her so, she's off in some world of her own. Let him go and play in his wife's lap. If he bows to her she'll be happy."

"What has Ravilal left undone to please his wife? When everything else failed, the poor fellow dared to ask me to say something to you. I hardly think he came to tell you, did he? Whatever—when your brother is begging you with folded hands, what would be the harm in saying a few words to his wife? Maybe she'll listen. It's not a good omen to always be having such quarrels."

"If everything goes wrong and collapses when such a low woman makes for bad omens, let it! It's not for fear of that. But now since you've talked to me, I don't want to hurt you, Rupa, and have your plan come to nothing," Mr. Sharma replied.

Mr. Sharma went himself and, knocking at his sister-in-law's door, spoke from outside. "For goodness' sake, what kind of behaviour is this of yours? Is it right for you not to be eating? Come have some food." Having uttered these words, he headed for his office.

Baral's daughter's sense of power was soaring; her spirit and bravura defied belief. She had put everyone else down. One person was left: her brother-in-law. Him, too, she would now deflate, and who could challenge her then? In the meantime Rupamati had come to get her up.

Her refulgence was something unseen! Pretending she could hardly walk, she came sobbing out of her room with great difficulty. Rupamati had to offer her support for going upstairs. Once she began to eat, ten handfuls of rice would probably not have been enough.

Madam Pandit had given up all intercourse with her younger daughter-in-law. She had no cause to complain, thanks to the good care taken of her by Rupamati. Sometimes, when women servants were lacking, housework piled up, yet Rupamati wouldn't let her mother-in-law do anything. "You're getting old. Is it right for us to see you work? It's time to think of higher worlds. Worship the gods with devotion. It will bring prosperity to us."

Thus Rupamati reasoned with her mother-in-law. The old woman beamed with delight. Oh, how fortunate she considered herself to have such an extraordinarily virtuous daughter-in-law, but when she saw her younger daughter-in-law's behaviour, her heart sank, and she felt as if she had fallen from the roof.

Rupamati's pregnancy reached seven months. She was no longer considered ritually pure. The cook prepared the curry himself for two or three days, but it was not tasty. Mr. Sharma, who was used to enjoying meals prepared by his wife with great love and toil, now faced difficulties. Rupamati sat nearby and offered advice, but Mr. Sharma's palate was not impressed. His mother stepped forward, thinking it wrong to make her son suffer.

It would have been difficult to call his mother's cooking insipid. After three or four days he got used to it. The turmoil with the younger daughter-in-law went on escalating. She would tell Ravilal, "We don't get curry to eat. How can I down rice and broth all the time?"

☙❧

Chapter 15

Today there was lots going on in Mr. Sharma's home. Everyone looked cheerful; everything was aglow. Friends who came to be part of the happy occasion were offering Mr. Sharma *dubo* grass.[99] Chattu even offered a coconut. The baby's face was very bright. It seemed to radiate auspiciousness. The Luintel family, hearing of the birth of Rupamati's jewel of a son, celebrated with utter delight. How could a holy man's prediction go wrong? It would be hard to describe Madam Pandit's joy when she saw the face of her grandson. To increase the happiness among his friends, her son had collected fifty-paisa, twenty-five-paisa and five-paisa coins for distribution. Madam Pandit was sent into raptures by comments from those who saw the child: "The eyes are just like its mother's." "The nose is like its father's." "Oh, what a rosy face!" "The forehead is broad too."

Others were furiously jealous, including many daughters-in-law who blushed with anger when they heard the praises heaped on their coeval as being a soaring example of good conduct. Husbands, in reproving their wives, cited this same ideal woman as a model, and mothers-in-law compared their daughters-in-law with her when they got mad. Being worthy and good is thus no guarantee of happiness; one becomes a target of others' jealousy. That is what happened to Rupamati. Few there were who, knowing her character and good fortune, did not feel pangs of misplaced envy. But no matter what other qualities she had, of what value were they? They had consoled themselves with the thought that the main glory of women is to give birth to a child. It was the one source of satisfaction, but fate had robbed them of this, too. Now what they could tell their husbands and parents-in-law? Everyone was happy. Only these women

---

[99] A sacred grass used on many festive occasions.

who were burning with jealousy affected an outward display of normalcy, and began to put on airs with the old lady.

Everyone's face was smiling; only the younger daughter-in-law was missing. Her person was not to be seen. She was lying balled up under a quilt in her bedroom, pretending to have a severe headache. Ravilal did everything to convince her. "So many people have gathered; the house is full. What can they be thinking about your being under a cloud? Don't be this way. Go upstairs once and show your face."

She refused. "Nobody cares about me here. I can't raise my head. My temples are burning, on fire! Let evil worms do their work. I won't be any the worse."

Painful "ow's" came from her mouth. Ravilal went upstairs resignedly, thinking that even if "Indra's father Chandra"[100] came, she wouldn't budge.

The Luintel family put their whole heart into gathering together everything the new mother and her baby needed. They sent twelve to fifteen day labourers with articles to brighten up their son-in-law's home. And what was prepared under the supervision of Luintelni Bajyai was nothing to turn up one's nose at. There was no shortage of food and drink. Other items aside, the homemade medicine their daughter took was of three or four varieties alone. Madam Pandit, seeing all this, burst with pride.

The celebration of the sixth-day ceremony also passed in grand fashion. All of Rupamati's relatives were invited. Her father and mother, offering five rupees each, feasted their eyes upon the face of their grandson. It was the first time they had dined at the daughter's home, and Mr. Sharma went out of his way to show his respect. Three castrated goats were slaughtered; ten different dishes of meat were prepared. This and the curried vegetables were cooked by the Brahmin. Everyone's mouth watered just smelling the aroma, and how they enjoyed getting their teeth into it! On that day Baral's daughter went upstairs.

---

[100] A Nepali proverb: Indra is the king of the gods, and even someone as powerful as his father would have no effect on the situation.

Even though the fires of jealousy were burning within her, it would have looked bad, as part of a joint family, to sit and do nothing.

Having satisfied the needs of all invitees and bid them good-bye, Madam Pandit placed the leftover meat and other items in the storeroom. Her elder son liked his rice with meat, but curry had also to be prepared every day. The leftovers from this curry, though, could be enjoyed at least for two or three days, and Madam Pandit covered them carefully so that the cat couldn't get at them. There was no one who did not eat their full that day, except the younger daughter-in-law, who went away after just a mouthful.

The next day the old woman got up a bit late. After taking a quick bath, she prepared a meal for the new mother, and then set about the domestic chores. She was at ease, knowing that she didn't have to cook curry that day, with the food from the day before to draw on. At mealtime she went upstairs. She arrived at the storeroom in a pant and looked in: the tasty dishes were all gone. There was neither roasted meat nor meatballs. Even the meat *achar* had vanished. Only one or two pieces of kabob were left—that and the untouched fried intestines. The sausages prepared by forcing the goats' blood into the fatty innards were also gone.

The old woman was abashed. How could the cat have gotten at things covered so tightly? It must, she thought, have been the work of a cat with two legs. A spring popped loose at not being able to feed her son; her eyes clouded over with anger. She began to roar so as to be heard downstairs. "Bahunnani, now there's nothing we can do! And I'm supposed to look on quietly? How can our house get on if things like this happen? When someone offers her food, she doesn't eat; she takes a mouthful, says she's not well and goes off. And now she's packed away this whole pile of meat! What's got into her? How can a person eat so much? I can't bear just sitting by and saying nothing. Things will go on like this as long as I stay in this cesspool. The only thing left is to smear ashes on myself and go into the forest. Can a house go on running when you can't trust people to keep their hands off things? There are nine laws of survival in this house—and it's survival of the fittest. What can we feed my son now? If we give him leftovers, there's no way of knowing whether the food has been touched or not.[101] If people up in the hills prepared such good food, they'd know what real eating is."

Baral's daughter heard everything. She had been grumbling at her sister-in-law's unwanted prosperity, holding her envy in check with great difficulty. Now she got the chance to unleash the fire raging within her against her mother-in-law. She reached upstairs in one breath and began quarrelling. "What did your father gobble down, you sinful old thing? Who are you to be levelling such charges? How can you say someone ate food from a locked storeroom? I'm supposed to be living off the wealth of an old witch like you? You're so hoity-toity you think the world couldn't run without you. Once I throw you out by the neck and send you on your way, you'll find out soon enough! If you're born in a house where you have nothing to eat but dried cabbage and cornmeal mush, how can you know about other homes? If I said every seven days we slaughtered a goat, it would look like boasting."

Her mother-in-law came back, "Who cares for such hollow blather? The fact is, things have disappeared from the storeroom. How could a cat lift such a big lid off a clay pot? Bahunnani, you tell me; who can talk sense with such cobbler women?"

As soon as the mother-in-law uttered the word "cobbler" the daughter-in-law grabbed her hand, saying, "Who are you to call me a cobbler?"

Madam Pandit pushed her away. Then the daughter-in-law's hand went for her hair. A tug started up. The old lady shouted, "My God, she's going to kill me!"

A great uproar ensued. Mr. Sharma came running. He looked and saw the pathetic goings-on. By the time Baral's daughter heard his voice, she had already withdrawn her hands, but she was still roaring. "You old

---

[101] Once food has been touched, it is considered impure for others' consumption.

woman, cholera couldn't get you, but you see what you're in for when you call others names?"

What could Mr. Sharma do? He was full of scorn. If enemies got the chance to mock, what would the neighbours say? How could he lay a hand on her, she being his sister-in-law? Rupamati was listening to everything from her corner. She grieved, but what to do? She couldn't come out. It was extremely disconcerting to see what troubles her mother-in-law was having while she had to confine herself for a couple of days.

Mr. Sharma sent for his brother. The latter was engaged in some illicit gambling. He came back and was told everything, but a word from his wife resparked the fire. "Is it right for her to call me a cobbler woman? Are you a cobbler for me to be called a cobbler's wife? Why should I remain silent after she's gone beyond all limits and stripped me of my caste like that? I socked her."

Upon hearing all this, Ravilal took up his wife's cause. He blamed his mother for beginning the quarrel, and told his brother frankly, "We're now to where Mother can't stand the sight of either of us. I've been thinking a lot. I'm the son who can't earn; my wife is the daughter-in-law who won't massage her legs. It's become impossible for us to stay in this house. I want to be separated."

For Mr. Sharma, it was just like falling down and finding oneself at one's destination, or being blind and finding an eye. The old woman could not say no either. What power could Rupamati exercise, having had no chance to discuss the matter with her husband?

The property was divided within three days in the presence of two or three friends. Ravilal became engaged in the search for a house. He found a narrow one with four rooms at Jhyabahal. The name-giving ceremony of his brother's baby had not even taken place, but his wife insisted that she would drink water in the new house even if she had to take it from the hands of an untouchable. What did she care about questions of defilement? They moved.

The old woman had not dreamed that her younger son would leave so abruptly. He had merely raised his voice in a fit of anger to boost his wife's cause. How could he abandon everything and go off? Seeing now that he really was splitting off from them, searching lodging and moving all his belongings, his mother felt her heart bleed. But she had not the strength to say anything. She wept to herself, but no words came from her mouth; what was there to say? Her son had now become his wife's one-man band. Whatever music she called for, he belted forth; he danced as she directed. He had lost his senses. If his senses hadn't been twisted, would he have blamed his own mother over his wife's trivial claims? Would he have kicked aside the home of his birth and upbringing?

It was natural that the old lady's heart felt pain. She had kept him nine months in her womb, looked after him with her whole heart in his youth, had forgotten about eating and sleeping when her children were sick, and visited temples to pray for their recovery; and during the suckling period she had maintained a strict diet, worrying that her son might fall sick from bad food. She had always loved her son, whether he did well or not, loved her or scolded her, and now, an able-bodied young man, he was leaving her, having cast blame on her falsely, in response to his wife's outpourings.

Only a mother's heart knows how much it hurts to see a son acting cruelly. And Madam Pandit loved her younger son ardently. She could never stand to see him gloomy. If he was she became disquieted. She did not tolerate anyone speaking out at him. If anyone so much as laid a finger on him, he had cried loudly. Then Madam Pandit would raise the roof. Nobody dared touch her son, either jokingly or in earnest. Whatever he did was taken in jest. She usually didn't believe the stories at all. Now all this came back to her, and she shed copious tears. Little wonder it was that her heart was greatly stricken.

Rupamati's heart, steeped in love and compassion, was thrown into turmoil by her brother-in-law's cruel and heartless blow. She had ever done her best, amidst her in-laws' trying ways, to prevent a split between her husband and his brother. Only she knew how much hardship she had had to undergo towards that end. How hurt she was when they left without saying a word to her or looking her in the face, only she herself knew.

Mr. Sharma also felt empty for three or four days. The brother he had loved so much as a child, who was born from the same womb, made of the same flesh and blood, nurtured on the same milk and brought up within the same walls, and who had caused him worry whenever he went somewhere—when today this brother had left home for good, it was natural that he should feel a sense of strangeness.

☙❧

Chapter 16

The name-giving and rice-feeding ceremonies[102] for Rupamati's son were held without further ado. Neither Ravilal nor his wife attended. Now Mr. Sharma's affairs had taken a turn for the better, thanks to his own efforts. And what could the Luintels do with so much property? They spent lavishly on the rice-feeding ceremony of their grandson. Rupamati had insisted that money not be thrown away on family frivolities. One should act in a way always in keeping with one's own nature. What good were those two days of colourful display? With such thoughts she tried to put a stop to things as best she could. But if her mother refused such a temperate regimen of spending, how would her mother-in-law agree? Her mother was ready to tighten her belt in order to meet all expenditures. Mr. Sharma would have nothing of it. Luintelni Bajyai nevertheless displayed the tenderness of a heart brimming with love by sending precious articles for the rice-feeding ceremony. Other things aside, the protective string[103] alone was entwined with a wealth of adjuncts. Now evil spirits, water and land sprites, demonesses, witches, succubi and headless ghosts couldn't lay a finger on the child.

On the other side of the family, once the move was made to the new house, all the responsibilities of a householder fell upon Ravilal. It was no easy thing either for Baral's daughter to keep things running smoothly. Merchants began to dun them, and wouldn't let up until the mistress of the house brought seven hundred rupees from home. It was out of the question to see her husband

---

[102] The name-giving ceremony occurs on the eleventh day following birth. The first rice is fed to a baby, in the case of girls, sometime after five months and, in that of boys, after six.

[103] The string tied around a baby during the rice-feeding ceremony. A small box or cloth containing gems and herbs is attached to it.

disgraced. Moreover, it was she herself who had encouraged him to split off from his family, so she dared not offend him.

She had spent all her dowry. Her mother's private property was also used up. She stole one diamond ring, two earrings and a pair of ear pendants from her mother's treasury. Poor Madhuvan knew nothing. Ravilal could now roam about with an expanded chest, having managed to dispose of the merchants. It was but natural that Baral's daughter felt bad when the coins were clinked down to pay them off, but when her belly began to swell, her hopes brightened, and she forgot about money worries. "We won't be the ones left out; we'll have a son too. The old woman's curse has kept me barren, but now she'll see just how fine we're doing," she said with head held high.

The question may be asked whether Chavilal's friends now kept vows of silence after such a misfortune had struck his family, and the answer would be that they did not. Just three days earlier a big gathering had been held at the house of his uncle,[104] Chattu Nepal. The latter's wife knew how to butter up people. She tugged at them like a magnet. She spoke so sweetly that even clever women didn't realize that their innermost selves were being drawn out. No one's children were allowed to go to her house, for once they were there she easily learned everything going on back home. Why, you couldn't count the women who envied her this trifling matter! Some were irked that not even mice came to them, whereas people flocked to this nobody. The reason the great number of people had assembled at their place on that particular day was to see Indrajatra. The old lady puckered her lips and began to speak.

Chattu's wife—"Our *subha*'s (Mr. Sharma had become a *subha*) sister-in-law is really a go-getter. All women should be like her, and then no one will dominate them. Her mother-in-law used to threaten her, so how could you expect her to just sit back? She pulled her hair

---

[104]His father's sister's husband.

something fierce. She got her husband to break with them and went to live in Jhyabahal."

Gamphe's sister-in-law now spoke up (who at the time had worked for Mr. Sharma)—"You're right about that, Madam! How quickly you understand people! From the seventh month of Rupamati's pregnancy on, the work started piling up for her old mother-in-law. The younger daughter-in-law didn't lift a finger. What the lady had to put up with! During the sixth-day ceremony Ravilal's wife really went overboard—obviously looking for an excuse to clear out. It's beyond understanding! She opened the storeroom with a matching key and had a lip-smacking meal of everything there was. Why should such a person have to put on a show the day before? A row broke out over it all. Things were said that shouldn't have been. And they went at each other's hair. The feeble lady must have felt it in her bones when that fool daughter-in-law slapped her. Luckily the elder son arrived, and that was that! Afterwards Ravilal came and raised the issue of living separately. His wife cast a spell on him with this one foxy maneuver."

Chattu's wife—"Okay, but why did Ravilal let himself be swayed that way? Bad actions mean bad intentions. Even though Chavilal couldn't come up with money, he did collect lots of household articles. Mr. Sharma divvied them up with great good will."

Gamphe's sister-in-law—"What can you say about such little things now? In any case, Mr. Sharma is educated and divided the stuff equally, as if his brother's share was a holy cow. No need for them to buy mattresses, pots and pans! If his brother behaved decently, he wouldn't need to worry about what to eat and what to wear, but you know his nature. How is such a spendthrift ever going to make it?"

Chattu's wife—"That Brahmin woman is there holding him by the hair. Do you think he can get away with anything under her?"

Gamphe's sister-in-law—"She has him under her control in more ways than one. But I'll tell you, if money doesn't come from time to time, she'd also be in a fix. Now she's done some wheedling and brought money from home, and also sold all her jewellery. How long can she keep up like that?"

Chattu's wife—"I heard lots of things were brought from Rupamati's parents' home for the rice-feeding ceremony."

Gamphe's sister-in-law—"I'm not up on that. I'd already left."

Chattu's wife—"Why did you leave so soon? Servants aren't looked kindly upon, I suppose—is it?"

Gamphe's sister-in-law—"Not so, Madam. I've tasted the food in many houses, but I haven't seen anywhere that treats its servants so lovingly. Granted, as long as the younger daughter-in-law was around, it was hard to take. Just fifteen days after I left was when the troubles began. The elder daughter-in-law is a real Lakshmi, Madam! For her, servants also have mouths, and a bit of all the curries should be given to them. Servants feel cold like everyone else, and should be provided with one or two warm covers. They should celebrate festivals and occasionally receive two or three paisa. There's so much I could say, Madam! There must be few people who understand the soul of the poor the way she does. I left only when people said that the wife of a driver shouldn't have to earn a living by scrubbing pots and pans."

Chattu's wife blushed. The other women were caught up in their own conversations. Some were reeling out a long account of themselves, some describing their sisters-in-law, some criticizing their daughters-in-law, some cursing their mothers-in-law, and some seeking the opportunity to tell Chattu's wife what their husbands had been up to with them. It was then that the procession came past. Everyone's attention turned to it.

Once the procession was by, discussion resumed for a while about Mr. Sharma's domestic affairs: The Luintels had pulled all the stops. Why did they have to offer five rupees apiece to see the child's face? Now what would people without that kind of money do? To get a daughter married you had to take out a loan, without leggings or cap to your name, in order to have something to lavish on your son-in-law. There was nothing under your mattress, yet only after promising nine outfits, a gold ring, chain and coin, a fashionable shawl and, for the bridegroom's procession, unlimited expenditures by the handful could you give your daughter away. How were you to get by? That the well-to-do had spoiled and finally dealt the death blow to time-honoured tradition was the main topic of discussion. Finally Rasbihari arrived and reduced everyone to silence with his ready replies.

Rasbihari—"What wild prey have you found today? Who's the talk about?"

Chattu's wife—"Didn't you hear about the Luintels' great feat? If they're rich, they're rich, but why pour their wealth into bringing endless trayfuls of things to their daughter for the rice-feeding ceremony? Are their heads so swollen over their wealth? They could do what they did because they were wealthy. So what's the big deal? How can they have the nerve to try to ruin others by introducing new customs?"

Rasbihari—"It's not good to cast blame uselessly. They have property and no other children—just this one daughter—and now after so many years they've got the opportunity to see a grandson; why shouldn't they celebrate with a happy heart? Why are you talking this way?"

Bachu's sister-in-law—"Do they have to give the baby a gold coin before feeding it rice? They could have given what they had to give in secret."

Chattu's wife—"That's what I said. Do they have the right to break tradition because they're rich?"

Rasbihari—"Of course they do! In society if one person rides a horse, should the next one try to ride an elephant? Whatever others do, follow the old ways and avoid imitating; then nobody can say anything—right? How have we fallen so low? By not copying good things from others and being all too eager to argue about unnecessary things. They have no son; all they have going for them is one daughter. They've got enough property, and in the end they'll have to put it in their daughter's son's name. Anyone who has four or five children shouldn't try to imitate them, even if they're rich. God has given everyone the power to use their conscience. Some let it rust by never using it, and where will that get them?"

Once Rasbihari got to discoursing no one could come back with any intelligent arguments. Everyone kept quiet. Even though he was sometimes flippant, he knew how to speak to the point.

৪০০৩

Chapter 17

Ravilal had had a pleasant time cavorting around at his brother's expense, but now that he himself had to shoulder all the burdens, things soon became phantasmagoric for him. His wife had given birth to a daughter. What panic the labour pains had been! Midwives and other helpers had been summoned. If their neighbour, a teacher, hadn't stepped in, Baral's daughter would have met her end. The due date had arrived; no preparations had been made. Money alone was of no use. Friends were needed, but friends were not enough either. Someone was needed who knew what they were doing.

Ravilal and his wife only had money. Ravilal told everyone that his wife would have been done for if her yelling hadn't wakened the teacher next door, since he himself had not been home that evening. It was a period during which he had let himself be drawn to one place or another at night, with stints of two or three days at home in between. Things were even harder for him after his wife had given birth. With great difficulty he found a Brahmin cook. It was enough work for her just looking after his wife, and he was left with the short end. By himself he was helpless. After a big scrap the diamond earrings his wife kept hidden ended up with the dealer Lal. The items could have fetched four hundred, but he let them go for three. It was enough to have a fling on for some days. Now that he had to run a household by himself, he needed something to run it on, but what did he care? His senses had left him, and why should they return?

How hard it was for his wife to keep the midwife's, cook's and maid's mouths sealed! "Cut your coat according to your cloth. Your hand is as free as it's ever been. What's your son going to eat and wear later on?"

His wife having thus raised the subject, he said, "'Once I'm dead let a low-caste be head. Who does the bearing can do the rearing.' I'm not giving up my fun."

"You've got no job. How can you carry on just roaming the back alleys the way you do? How long do you plan to gad about without finding a position? You don't suppose I can always be bringing money from my parents' home, do you? You should have heard my sisters-in-law grumbling this year. And then my mother got taken ill. Once she's out of action my sisters-in-law won't thread a needle for you. Someone else's daughter isn't your own. Why haven't you gotten that into your head yet?"

His wife roared. Ravilal would just wordlessly ignore her. His condition worsened by the day. "Take your time; let it be a son"[105] was the maxim Baral's daughter followed. Day and night she poured body and soul into seeing it come true. If one was pure in heart, God would answer prayers. She gave birth four times within three years. Four daughters were the result. Their maternal grandmother took the first and third of this string of girls in with her. It was difficult enough for Baral's daughter to bring up even two of them. Who knows what would have happened if she had had to bring up all four!

The pregnancies had already turned her into a wreck, lacking as she did good care. After only a month she was back at work. Illness laid her up; her earlier energy and drive were gone. Her husband hid out with his bhang gang. Now even his eyes had gone red. Without a half pound of *peda*s he couldn't go to bed. There wasn't a year in which he didn't blow two or three hundred rupees on gambling. Whatever jewels and ornaments had been in the house were now in hock at the government loan office. There was not a single paisa worth of income. It would not have been hard to manage plain household expenses, but the number of children went on increasing. Her husband's ways had become hopeless. If he was not provided money on demand, he made life impossible for

---

[105] A common Nepali proverb indicating the importance attached to male offspring.

her. With things the way they were, destruction was nigh at hand.

Baral's daughter, feeling very sick, made up her mind to go home. Ravilal was happy to see her leave. For one thing, she never came back from her parents' home empty-handed. Secondly, there would be no one at home to grumble; he could do whatever he liked and go wherever he wanted. He could expand his chest and say valiantly, "Enjoy life!"

Once Baral's daughter arrived in Chepetar, her sisters-in-law turned into chickens that had eaten salt. Her outbursts intimidated them; no one had the courage to say a word. Their mother-in-law was a formidable person, too. The day had yet to come when she would have a heart-to-heart talk with them.

And then their sister-in-law was a mother-in-law to beat all mothers-in-law—one to make even her own mother-in-law dance. What a phenomenon she was! Now cousins on both sides of the family were gathered under the same roof. Terrible fights broke out over the children. The old lady had the peculiar trait of loving her daughter's offspring more than her sons'. If she tossed off homemade cotton clothes on the latter, the former had to have alpaca. If meat and other delicacies were prepared, she lavished them boundlessly on her daughter's daughters. If her son's children spoke up, she'd begrudge them one or two pieces without saying a thing. If she cooked a lesser amount, they wouldn't even get a whiff of it. Given such excesses, it was no wonder that the daughters-in-law were exasperated.

Madhuvan's youngest son had a son. The grandfather decided to conduct a fancy name-giving ceremony for this first-born offspring in order to silence criticism among the ranks. The village women, having a chance to do this man of wealth a favour, gathered throughout his house. It was a splendid affair. But then Ravilal's third daughter fell sick, and the name-giving came to a halt. Madhuvan was at a loss; his wife couldn't do a thing, she being afraid of her daughter, and he of her. Those able to curry the daughter's favour got hold of some *achar* and other food items; of the remaining things, some ended up in the stomachs of Baral's daughter and her children, and others rotted and were thrown away. With the mother-in-law rankling over her youngest daughter-in-law, what chance was there for the ceremony to go ahead in style? Four Brahmins were called upon to finish the work with no frills.

Baral's daughter, her boldness now snapped, took to bed. Previously she used to spend one or two months before returning. This time months came and went without a sign of her. The time passed nicely for Ravilal, his wife having left behind thirty to forty days of provisions. After that, though, the day of reckoning drew nigh. His friends and buddies began to drop by his home. He had no one to fear. Party after party was held. House and fields were mortgaged one after the other. The money owed to confectioners, fruit sellers, Muslims and other dealers in meat went on accumulating. Kabuli vendors had the opportunity to sell some more pomegranates and dried fruits.

The year had been a disaster for Baral's daughter. She had had to spend most of her time convalescing at her parents' home. Her mother was not in good shape either, suffering as she did from asthma. The daughter saw with her own eyes how her mother's hands and legs had swollen. The thought that if something happened it would be the end—that even finding something to drink would be difficult—set a shaman's drum beating in her heart. If it was as hard as it was living with only two daughters at home, what would it be like with all four? The more she considered her future, the more she felt frightened. She thought that by scrounging around in the till, she could come up with five hundred rupees' worth of goods, now that the price of gold was up. But if even Kubera's treasury[106] could be drawn too heavily upon and depleted, how long would her mother's hold out, when every year she had made off with a fine stash? On top of that, Madhuvan's family had become very big. More than twenty pounds of rice had to be cooked for one meal. Then too, it wouldn't be exaggerating to say that there

---

[106]Kubera is the overseer of the gods' wealth.

was not a single day at home without some festival or another. What cash, then, would there be floating about? The six or seven thousand they had was tied up in business. There was not a thing in the house. Nobody knew what was going on.

Baral's daughter arrived home. Neighbours came running to tell her about her husband's various pursuits.

Kajini—"This time, Madam, we had many sleepless nights. If it had been Shivaratri or Krishnastami,[107] we would have acquired much merit. Not just a day or two—every day your room was turned into a rumble den. Sometimes you heard 'Hah-hah! Hah-hah!', sometimes 'Hee-hee! Hee-hee!' And sometimes there were hymns to repurify our ears. What else? It would be impossible to describe everything."

Nanicha—"Yes, Madam! Sometimes they talked about religious things; we were amazed."

Baral's daughter—"How long did it go on like that?"

Kajini—"Maybe about a month. They shouted and nigh on raised the roof. The cook skipped off ten or twelve days after you went back home. She had to wait for hours to serve rice to your husband. What could she do just sitting around? Another Brahmin was brought in. The man was a crook: instead of looking after his master, he gave him the shaft. As soon as he heard you were coming, he ran away. Who knows what all he made off with? This same Brahmin used to spend wads of money for this, that and the other dish. What a profit he must have made! Your husband was bamboozled."

Nanicha—"Some days back a tall, fearful-looking man with baggy trousers and turban was calling your husband from the courtyard."

Baral's daughter—"Who would spend money that way just to gab and have a good time? I made a rough estimate before leaving. His friends must have chipped in. And how much could they have spent on food?"

Kajini—"What do you mean, Madam? What do Kusicha, Syakhu, Jhilke and Dhanamane ever have on

---

[107]The festival in August-September celebrating the birth of Krishna. On both holidays devotees customarily hold vigils.

them? Where would they get money from? And if they didn't have some fun, why would they have come swarming like bees? What are you saying?"

The more Baral's daughter heard, the more she felt herself slipping into the grave. On the other hand, she couldn't afford not to hear them out. Her stomach was turning cartwheels, and she was in no mood to speak, so that it was with great difficulty she said, "Did they sing hymns to Lord Narayan while sinking their hands into some meat curry, or do something else of that sort?"[108]

Nanicha—"Which day was it, Kajini?" As soon as these word were uttered Kajini gave a wink. She signalled her to keep quiet by putting her finger to her mouth. Nanicha didn't understand; she went on blithely. "You mean the dancing?"

Baral's daughter blushed, lowered her gaze and asked in a low voice, "What kind of dancing? Why this silence, Nanicha? Speak up."

Nanicha—"Kajini knows."

Now Kajini had no choice but to speak. Thinking it no use to hide what would come out one way or the other anyhow, she let the details be heard.

Kajini—"Yes, Madam! It was seven days ago. A trained dancer from some palace, with a sweet voice and very good at dancing. She danced with small tinkling bells around her ankle. Not that beautiful . . . middle-aged. She charged sixty rupees for dancing three hours. Ram! Ram! Such shameless women! I wonder that she's able to prance about among men. Like a live wire. Where did they find out about her? Sixty rupees down the drain for one session! They'll have nothing on their backs in no time! Wasn't it the same day, Nanicha, we heard Jhilke clapping his hands and shouting, 'They say nymphs' dancing is good, but could it be as good as hers?' There were marvels galore that day: they knocked off several kilos of pomegranates and apples, Gangaram's *laddu*s, *chamcham*s from Naxal, Brahmacha's *ghevar*s, Siddha's cakes and Maharaja's *rasgulla*s.[109] Five kilos of meat were

---

[108]The devotees of Vishnu (Lord Narayan) do not eat meat.
[109]Different types of sweets.

picked up from the butcher; that, too, gone in no time. Orders were sent to where good-quality stuff is made, and names must have been recorded in the account book."

While this talk was going on Chattu's wife arrived from somewhere or other. "My dear, your husband has ruined everything! The rumour is that he's put all his property up as security with Chunche. Yesterday Rasbihari was telling me that. He's spent his life dredging up others' secrets. He wouldn't have said such a thing without being absolutely sure. I didn't sleep the whole night—wide awake the whole time. I heard you had come and came to let you know. What are you going to do? There's no way to escape fate. But don't let it get you down."

When Baral's daughter heard this, her mouth and throat went dry. Her vision blurred. After a while she began to stare at her daughters. Now what awful plight would the four be in? How would they get them married off? How would they perform all the customary acts? With such thoughts to entertain, it wouldn't be long before madness set in, so what wonder was it that Baral's daughter's face was drawn? She had dived into just such an ocean of thought.

The great pandit Ravilal Sharma arrived back home after a trip to Dakshinkali with his group of merrymakers. He did not know that his wife and children had come. He entered the house humming loudly. Having ascended but one step, he saw the porters, and his heart sank. The colour in his face came out, and he felt like collapsing right on the spot, even as his hands and legs weakened and he began to sweat profusely. The narcotic of pleasure he had succumbed to made heels. His wife and daughters began to dance in front of his eyes. Now that the day of reckoning had come, wasn't it time to try to control himself? Now that the rest of his family was back in mind, wasn't it time to come to his senses? Who cared?

For a moment he was worried how he would face his wife and daughters. Slowly he approached. He couldn't raise his head to his wife. The wound in Baral's daughter's heart from hearing about the goings-on was still fresh; it had not healed. She had no wish to see her husband. She remained stiff-necked and long-faced—in a turmoil at the thought of the fix they were in, and whether all their secrets had been spilled. For that reason she, too, was unable to utter a word. And then his second daughter asked, "Daddy, why have you become so thin?" That startled him, but even then he had not the courage to reply.

A bad habit is like an addiction. During the time you're high on it, you don't notice anything else. As the effect wears off, little by little your senses return, and you realize the state you're in: "My God, what a messed-up life I'm leading!" you say. You resolve not to indulge again, but when the group of friends gets together, the craving returns. You try to stop it but it won't stop; there's no reining in a mind bent on self-indulgence. You take the plunge, are trapped and stuck in place. Try a hundred thousand times and rack your brains—it's no use. From this you start thinking you can't get rid of a bad habit once it's there, but that's not true; it's just difficult to learn good habits after you get used to bad ones. Only if you could consciously control yourself when in a normal state, or else if you could keep company with some great master able to sway others' hearts and dispense wisdom, or fall into the hands of experienced psychologists—only then would you make the passage; otherwise it would be extremely hard to get on well.

Now this was the very state Ravilal had arrived at. He had become a horrid wretch from his ill association with the street crowd. Everybody felt it would be quite impossible to reform him now. Now when his daughter called him "Daddy," he experienced a jolt. It was a rude awakening. The tough questions of life began gnawing away at him. He tried to look at his daughters but couldn't; his eyes were dazzled. A sense of hopelessness overcame him. He had no power of speech. He wanted to express his love for his daughter but couldn't raise his hands. He looked toward his wife's face and saw despair and hopelessness suddenly appear on it. His features drooped; their eyes did not meet.

Just then a voice came from the courtyard. "Mr. Sharma! Where's Mr. Sharma?"

When he heard that voice, Ravilal's face changed colours. Horrified, he instructed his daughter, "Go and tell him I'm not at home."

And that's what the poor child said. "My daddy says to tell you he's not at home."

"Oh, he'll kill me, and that'll be it if he finds me. He won't let me drink even water. They'll bind me hand and foot, and I'll have to stay on the ground floor of his house in this cold." He was in agony.

Luckily the man from Kabul didn't understand that the child's word's contained a secret. He thought Ravilal was not at home. "We're sure to meet one of these days, and then we'll show him what's what." He raised a warning finger.

Ravilal had not the courage to sit around with his family long. He went to his room, slammed the door and lay down on the bed face-up with limbs splayed. "Now the shopkeepers are getting on me. I wonder how much my wife brought bundled up with her. A little will not be enough this time. It'll be hard to keep them quiet without a large sum."

Wave upon wave of such thoughts rose in his mind. Again a voice could be heard shouting from the courtyard. "Mr. Sharma! Where has Mr. Sharma gone? I need money for four goats. Up to now he hasn't paid."

As no response was forthcoming, the yelling went on all the more insistently. Now it was the meat-sellers from Sundhara! No one surpassed them in creating an uproar. There was no way for Baral's daughter not to look out the window. "Who are you? Are you trying to ruin my ears? You've already been told my husband's not home, so why all the fuss?"

"Okay, we'll nab him on the outside and then teach him a thing or two for taking meat from us." With that they left.

Seeing those red-eyed Muslims like messengers from the underworld, Baral's daughter, too, became frightened. "Oh Lord, how are we going to get out of this mess? There must be something in my previous life there shouldn't be to get caught in such a tangle." She began to wail.

Thus the day passed. In the evening she had dinner and went to bed. There had been no occasion for a conversation between husband and wife.

From the next day on Ravilal was scared to go out. One day he was sitting in the drawing room. Gange's son came and went directly upstairs. How could he have done otherwise? No one gave him the time of day if he went to the courtyard and called from there. It was always "He's not at home." How long would it go on like this? Arriving upstairs, whom should he find but Ravilal! "What's been happening, Mr. Sharma? I came many times but didn't catch you. I need the money for the *laddus*."

"Your money is not going anywhere. Come tomorrow and collect it," Ravilal said, but the boy wouldn't take no for an answer. He sat down on the floor. Ravilal didn't have the courage to ask for money from his wife. He should have paid about five rupees for the *laddus*, but the man demanded seven, thinking that he could cheat such a person. There was no getting around paying the seven rupees. Two weeks earlier he had acquired five phonograph records on loan from the shop of a Muslim; these he thrust upon the boy and sent him away.

From that day on Ravilal left off staying in the drawing room and took up quarters on the top floor. His friends and buddies ceased gathering the way they had before. Do bees congregate about flowers with no nectar? Who cared for faded petals? Two old men from the neighbourhood had used to visit Ravilal to listen to his gossip, but even they couldn't hold out. Hearing them coughing one day, a Muslim staked out the premises, thinking the owner must have been home, and it was with great difficulty that he could be driven away. Since that day he had not wanted them to come. And why should they keep on coming if not welcome? Businessmen for their part did not want to see Ravilal smoking his hookah.

One day the sweet-seller from Naxal made an appearance. Ravilal's daughter told him that her father had just gone out; by now all family members were well trained in telling lies. But he heard the hookah gurgling. "Do you think your lying will make me go away. Isn't that the sound of tobacco I hear? Was it nice munching on the *chamcham*s? Am I now supposed to crack my teeth getting you to pay? I had to leave work to come get twelve rupees. Now I'm not moving a foot without first collecting up," he said firmly.

Baral's daughter could not tolerate her husband's constant degradation. She began to make a pitch and gather people to the cause. When houses around the courtyard heard loud voices, they emptied onto it, whence she scraped up fifteen rupees and clinked them out. She sent someone to ask her husband how much he owed, but he didn't know the figure. "He's honest, not the cheating type. Give him what he says. It won't make any difference."

Oh, what a lush! How many sweets did he take? How many times was it? How much was left to pay? He had no idea??? Could such a person support his family? What a fix he'd be in if he had to make it on the outside! How could such a person keep his family going? All these question rose in the mind of Baral's daughter.

Ravilal for his part felt renewed hope from his wife's having paid the fifteen rupees. "If I could pay off all my loans, it would be low-down to take a loan again! Great God, I confess. If I do this once more, every last thing will be gone. I should renounce the world and take to the jungle like a yogi with tongs and Shiva's name on my tongue."

Ravilal thundered so that his wife could hear. Sometimes he reeled off solemn pledges: "I'll eat beef before getting into bad company again. I'll become a sweeper if it means getting a job. Just get me out of this and I'll be a monkey's son if I don't earn some money." Every oath under heaven came out of his mouth.

One day the Muslim goat-seller came and created a stir. He jumped up and down in the courtyard as if all hell had broken loose. Baral's daughter looked from the window and asked, "What are you roaring about? My husband isn't home."

"My foot, he's not! I've come ten times without meeting him. Now I'm not moving one step until I get the money out of him," the Muslim replied.

"Go and lay hands on the person who bought the goat," Baral's daughter said, but the Muslim didn't listen; he remained fixed in place. Ravilal lay quietly lest his presence be noticed. He had even given up putting water in the hookah. If he had to go downstairs he trod softly, like a cat. This was how Ravilal passed his days.

॰ॐ॰

Chapter 18

Today there was lamentation in the home of Madhuvan. Who could bear to see the agitation of Ravilal's two daughters? They were overcome by the death of their grandmother. The eldest daughter had reached marriageable age and acquired much discernment. The daughters-in-law were no less distraught. Their weeping and sobbing went on for a long time, before gradually subsiding. Household affairs came hurtling down upon them. Pandit Madhuvan tied the key to the treasury to the sacred thread around his chest.

A few days after the mourning period, having to retrieve the nose ornament given as collateral by Latte, who had come to claim it, he opened the box but couldn't find it. He searched for the diamond ring, earrings and other things, and discovered that a host of mounted glitters was gone. He almost lost consciousness. He felt alarmed and dizzy, his lips turned dry, pearls of sweat formed, his heart palpitated, and his body grew stiff. He was at a loss for words. Putting his hand to his head, he descended to his haunches and then fell on his back. The whole world looked black. What to do now?

How would he deal with his debtors? If they claimed three *tola*s of gold for one *tola* given, what would he say? A total of about ten *tola*s was missing. It was almost impossible to assess the value of the diamonds and pearls. Some had been inherited by his father, and others sold to him by a Burmese who had found them among Delhi loot, but in any case they were shiny and shimmery, and looked very expensive. As Madhuvan recalled this and felt remorse, tears began to flow. Seeing that all had fallen apart, he cursed himself. "What a fool I was for saying nothing after seeing my wife hand over things to our daughter! I should have checked from time to time or tried to keep the key out of her hands. It would have been all right had the butter dropped into the butter pot, but my son-in-law finished everything. Only some days back my daughter sent the bad news. It's gotten to where he can't go anywhere for all the businessmen he's cheated. His home and land have already been mortgaged. Everything has gone wrong. My own house is ruined, and my daughter is in the same fix. What greater fool than me can there be in this world?"

He tried to set foot out of his treasure room, but his legs shook at the thought of facing his sons and daughters-in-law. They were the ones who had said that his wife had spoiled their daughter by lavishing things on her. That time he had kept mum—when he had seen her ways and felt a shiver. He should have looked more deeply and got to the bottom of the matter. Tough times loomed. The poor man became like a chicken that had eaten salt. For some time now his loan business had been heading steadily downhill. About three or four thousand rupees were outstanding; two or three thousand remained—and that only if all the articles in the treasury could be sold.

Gradually Madhuvan's sons and daughters-in-law came to know about the state of affairs. They guessed from his look and behaviour. Their nieces soon became hideosities to their eyes. The younger aunt had been languishing ever since the name-giving ceremony of her son. She left nothing unsaid. No one in the house who saw their plight stood up for them with kindness or sympathy. So long as their grandmother had been alive no one had dared to say a thing to them; she turned everyone inside out. Now even the children of their uncles looked for excuses to snap at them. The latter could no longer hold their heads straight. Though they were children, it was hard for them, who were used to sweet food, now to have to digest rough fare. Sometimes, if they had a hankering for something, they were treated to obscene gestures. "Your mother made off with everything. What's left to eat now? Here, take that!"

When Baral's daughter heard that her mother had taken leave of this world, she felt as if a mountain had come crashing down on her. She lost her senses. Her face paled. She tried to cry but tears would not come out; a fire flamed within. Sleepless nights were spent pacing up and down in front of her bed at the unbearable pain of domestic affairs. How could she remain steady when such misfortunes came one after the other? Her husband's behaviour was the same. When an accounting was made, he was found to have spent ten thousand rupees. Seven thousand were lost to gambling, and some three to four thousand in paying back shopkeepers.

Now that she was back from months at home, it was the same old story: not a single day in which the shopkeepers didn't raise a ruckus. On top of that, all the landed property and jewellery were pledged out as security. She went to check up on her jewellery and didn't find any. There were marriages to arrange for her four daughters. The eldest was already thirteen, and they were getting a bad name for themselves all around for allowing her to mature beyond the age of wedlock. It had been the mother's hope that her own parents would arrange marriages for two of her daughters. That hope was shattered with her mother's death. Was it likely that she could now come to terms with her sisters-in-law? How would she survive? Baral's daughter was in dire straits.

Ravilal began to have fits when loans were not paid by her. Sometimes having sat down to eat, he set plates flying because there was too much salt in the curry; sometimes he slapped his youngest daughter for having tarnished his pipe. Sometimes he would say, "Okay, you baggage, if you've got money, out with it; otherwise you're in for worse than a black dog!"

"That's all hot air. What do I have to give? Whatever I had, you've finished off. I've already suffered what there is to suffer. What suffering can you cause me now? Kill me; I'm as good as dead already. Dying would be better than having to put up with your grumbling day and night. Why can't I just die? Why does God take away someone who's got everything, and not me? Death is balm to the weary." She began to cry.

One day Ravilal received word of the arrival of a sitar player at Premman's. That day the born gallant who enjoyed his flings had been having to keep low for fear of the shopkeepers. When he heard of Premman's entertainment programme, he couldn't control himself. He arrived, deciding to take the consequences, no one being likely to meet him at night. The sitar began to play. He sat inconspicuously in a corner of the drawing room, covering his face with a thin quilt. Only his nose and eyes were visible. No one recognized him easily.

Lalpari's fingers danced over the strings of the sitar. What a lovely tone! What a dulcet hand! The people listening began to sway. Some clapped to the tune, and others shouted "Bravo! Right on!"—this to inspire the performer. Ravilal, too, was charmed. How could he keep himself cooped up in a corner? It became intolerable; there was no enjoyment if he could not see the sitar and clap to the tune himself. He girt himself up and went forward. Up till then few had recognized him. Upon seeing him, they all expressed delight. "Ravilal!" Now everyone expected the concert to reach its climax. The sitarist, too, was pleased to see her old friend. It was then that a Muslim suddenly arrived in the courtyard. The summons "Mr. Sharma!" was uttered, and a face shrivelled and turned blue. Ravilal covered himself with the quilt and began to quail.

The Muslim had brought two or three friends, and together they raised a howl in the courtyard. The sitar concert came a close. Poor Premman had secretly organized the concert; his heart began to pound with fear that all hell would now break loose, for the Muslims were bent on making a scene. When he tried to find out how the curs had come by their information, it emerged that it was the work of Ravilal's old bosom friend Jhilke. The ingrate had acted treacherously! And Premman was in no position to hide anybody. The Muslims may have been walking along the main road and stumbled across the sitar concert by accident, and thinking that their defaulter might be hiding out there had raised a stir. Premman asked Ravilal to leave.

No sooner did Ravilal reach the ground floor than he was surrounded. "Mr. Sharma, maybe you could tell us when we'll be getting the money for the records?"

Ravilal gave a quick reply. "Why, anytime you want."

Muslim—"We've been to your home a hundred times, and always we hear 'Not here.' Now we won't leave you."

With that they seized hold of Ravilal and took him to their own lodgings, blocked the exit and played cat and mouse with him. When the news reached his wife, she pretended not to hear. Her heart, already hardened, would not have melted in any case. If she had shelled out even the little money required for his release, how would they fill their stomachs? They had reached the point where not a grain of rice came in, all their fields having already been mortgaged. When messengers came from Ravilal one after the other, she showed them her palms and sent them away. Not a single grey hair did she have to give.

Ravilal was raving mad. In the first place, he was confined to the cold ground floor, and on top of that the place, next to the latrine, was a stench. Others didn't enter the room without holding their nose. How distressful it was for him! "Just let me get out of here and I'll whip her to death." With such words he assuaged his anger.

Things had been looking up in Mr. Sharma's house ever since the day Ravilal and his wife had left. Income was on the rise. Sickness and sorrows found no entry. The old lady was caught up in playing with her grandson. She wouldn't set him down even for a moment. She carried him around and guided his walking. If the child showed its teeth, she joined cheeks with it, saying, "That's my boy! What a beautiful smile you have!" If at times it came out with some inarticulate sound, she would jump for joy and exclaim, "Why, you know how to talk!" Her legs forgot what the floor felt like. If at other times it cried during her worship, she put a spoonful of sacred water in its mouth and so pacified it. When someone made the child cry, she lost her senses. Sometimes she carried on conversations with it by herself. In this way she had been spending the days happily. She remembered her younger son only occasionally. She would shed tears at the thought of his cruel and harsh treatment. Otherwise she had forgotten all past woes.

Mr. Sharma was in high spirits. His office work was going smoothly. No one could say a word against him. There were no problems at home either. The Lakshmi-like Rupamati was managing all household affairs very well. She lacked nothing and basked in her husband's love. She kept herself busy serving him. Thinking that her brother-in-law might be in distress, she made inquiries about him. Now when she heard of the indignities the Muslims had subjected him to, her heart went out to him. Without telling her husband she sent twenty-five rupees. If she had found out earlier, the poor fellow would not have had to undergo such hardship. At last his skin was saved.

Ravilal went home directly and began to fulminate. "Where has your brain gone? If you take a loan, there's no way not to pay it back. Once you had to shell out ... if you had got the Muslim off my back a few days earlier, I wouldn't have had to be stuck on that cold ground floor! Those fools were out to kill me!"

Baral's daughter was surprised at her husband's words. Unable to make head or tail of them, she knew not what to reply. She had not loosened her purse strings, but if she was getting credit for having done so, why deny it? But who these days would have had the kindness of heart to pay? It was a cause for great wonderment. Such thoughts rose in her mind.

Just then a shopkeeper came roaring up. "Mr. Sharma, where have you been? It's now three months I haven't received the money for the *ghevar*s." He began to cause a commotion in the courtyard.

"What a fool! Why should he be crying like a banshee? It's enough to split my eardrums." Ravilal came down from the top floor. He was aggravated that his wife had said nothing. The merchant wouldn't let up. He thought that by threatening him in front of his neighbours, he would get him to say, Okay, okay—settle down! He had no intention of leaving without the money.

"Why are you giving me crap over four rupees? On the one hand, you pride yourself on being the daughter of rich folk. Don't you have any shame? As long as I lived I thought no one would have reason to mock me, and then my life would amount to something. This is utterly disgusting! It's two hours now he's been shouting." Hearing these words from Ravilal's mouth, his wife was unable, try as she did, to control their laughter.

Homiletics is a characteristic feature of vagabond society. Go where it gathers and listen to Vedanta philosophy, or if you need someone to give teachings engage one of them, and he'll be able to assemble subject matter from up and down the country. Ravilal was like that. He was a renowned man of experience among such society—great at fashioning masterful speeches and full of knowledgeable talk, but what was it all worth when he was unable to put words into action? His nature ran counter to his discourse. There was not a shameless person like him around. Was it any wonder that his wife was dazed by his brilliant talk? She sent the merchant on his way with the four rupees.

☯︎

Chapter 19

Baral's daughter's days were passing very unhappily. Now it was hard to find scraps of food, let alone a decent meal. Not a grain of rice was to be had anywhere.

There was no income—not a clipped paisa's worth. She had buried three to four hundred rupees under the ground floor. That much was left. Once she started using a little of it daily, how long would it last? She began to manage things with great thrift. She made jar upon jar of *gundruk*. This she cooked up into curries. It was mean pickings for Ravilal. How could a mouth unsatisfied with a single grain of rice unless accompanied by a good broth be expected to imbibe *gundruk* stock? And there was only this one kind of curry. Ravilal became thinner and thinner. His behaviour also changed completely. Before, his wife had been a cow that fulfilled all wishes, and so held in high esteem. She had definitely been a help. If she was piqued and money not forthcoming, he used to play the wolf, smearing her body with turmeric and reaping a heap of coins. But now her supply of money had disappeared. With the death of his mother-in-law the main source had dried up. He began to rebuke her for even the smallest things. If she so much as peeped, he intimidated her fiercely. Now that his sweet tooth and free hand had had to cut back, his brain had lost some of its balance. He would jump up saying, "You've got your hand on money, so out with it! You won't kill me this way!"

One day she cooked up a dish of *gundruk* and a curry of plain vegetables. He went to the kitchen and sat down, and seeing the rice and curry he averted his eyes. He said, "You witch! You're close to killing me, cooking such awful food!"

She snapped back, "If your tongue is so particular, you need to earn some money. You're always expecting to live off my property. Aren't you the least bit ashamed? Where am I supposed to come up with anything now? My parents' home is barely getting by. No matter how much they give—and they've been shelling out—it's always the same mess! Now that my mother is gone, where will the money come from? Nowhere!"

"Don't give me lip, you whore! A dog couldn't digest this ghee. You're a disgrace to me, living in my house."

"How can you say your house? It's more like Tunche's."

No sooner were these words out of her than he went to the kitchen, grabbed her by her plait, and twisted and kicked her about. In his anger at the tasteless food, he said, "Are you trying to show disrespect—talking sass?"

"My God, he's killing me! Somebody help!" his wife howled.

Their neighbour the teacher came running and separated them.

"I won't stop until I kill this whore. The witch! Because of her I've had to live apart from the mother who bore me. I had to break off relations with a loving sister-in-law. She got me into quarrels with my brother, who was a god to me." Ravilal was gnashing his teeth. The teacher appealed to him, and got him to go downstairs.

Baral's daughter was now undergoing unspeakable hardship. Ravilal disappeared for five or six days; no one knew where he was or what he was imbibing. Rumour had it that he was in with a group of yogis on the banks of the Bagmati. How he survived, nobody knew. One day the man from Kabul ran into him at Tripureshvar. Upon seeing him, Ravilal floundered. When the man said, "What's the problem, Mr. Sharma?" he could barely come back with a reply.

"I've been to Calcutta. I just got back the other day."

But the man from Kabul saw through him, from the appearance he made. And his experience with him had not been the best. He had been to his house a hundred times, and nobody had told him that he was away in Calcutta. Lies never did sound right. "Yes, I know, you rascal! I won't let you out of my sight a minute until I have my money. And with that he dragged him off.

The parade ground exercises at Tundikhel had just finished, and the soldiers enjoyed listening to the man from Kabul roar. But when they saw Ravilal's attire, they were dumbstruck: an embroidered cap, woollen coat, woollen muffler, fine woollen undercoat and trousers, Dick's Company shoes, woollen socks, a handkerchief smartly sticking out of his pocket, his hair stylishly cut, and his moustache well trimmed on both sides. There was no one who, looking at him, wouldn't have said that he was a proper Brahmin or Kshatriya. That was all the more reason for people to gather to see such a person being disgraced. Few indeed are those who do not enjoy watching others quarrelling and being dishonoured.

By now people were cutting jokes. "Look at that highfalutin rascal—been sitting on the Kabuli's money for a year. Look at his get-up! If you can cheat a shopkeeper, why not enjoy life? If we could get our thrills on other people's money, we'd be doing it too. He probably has just a straw mat at home, but look at his outfit here!"

"Hey Kabuli, where are you taking this fellow?"

Ravilal had to listen to all this silently. He did not utter a word, thinking that the abuse would only increase if he did any squirming in the man's grip. He walked meekly. Then suddenly, at the power authority headquarters, his eyes fell on his brother. The latter, wondering whom the Kabul man was hauling past in the midst of a bustling crowd, looked, and it was his own brother. Whatever may have come between them, it was but natural for his heart to grieve at his brother's ill fortune.

Today he was forced to witness with his own eyes what Rupamati had prophesied. If his brother had acted properly, he would have been lacking for nothing. "For God's sake, don't do anything. Just stay quietly at home. Don't bring disgrace to the family name," he had begged, but it didn't sink in. Ravilal, having succumbed to his wife's beguilements, did things that shouldn't have been done and said things that shouldn't have been said. The vainglorious nobody who had said that he was being forced to live beneath his status—look where that got him! Today how the colour had disappeared from his face when he saw his brother! No happiness had ever come by treading the path he had chosen. He had spent his childhood stealing. Prostitutes and gambling ruined him in his youth. He was at the end of his tether, and still he was no wiser. No, his brain was full of straw—every last nook and cranny of it!

Swept along by this train of thought, Mr. Sharma reached home without even noticing how he crossed the street. No sooner did he arrive on the first floor than Rupamati came to welcome him with a sweet and loving smile. She was startled to see her husband so grave but kept quiet, thinking it unwise to speak up. In the end Mr. Sharma himself broached the subject.

Mr. Sharma—"You warned us, Rupa! Today I had to face the sorry plight of seeing what that number one fool and hen-pecked brother of mine has got himself into. From what he was wearing, you'd have thought he has thousands of rupees at home. Disgusting! What an ass he is! The more I think of him, the madder I get."

Rupamati was distressed at her husband's words. She was frightened to think that her brother-in-law's end was in sight—that her ears would now not have much more to hear. Mr. Sharma continued.

Mr. Sharma—"Doesn't he know he has to pay back money he takes from other people? And what does the devil do but take loans from those Kabulis! For one thing, they charge three or four times more, and then once they collect all that interest—what do you think? They bring all their stuff from their own country! First, they're sure to bring nice new, strange things. When they've sold them, they get articles from the local businessmen and sell them. Anything they touch is considered good. These days people have become sly. Didn't you hear? The goat-sellers at Sundhara bring hill goats and say they're from the plains. They have fun cheating. Businessmen have to make a profit by hook or by crook, but these fools are something else! Why do they go to them?"

Rupamati—"I don't know if I agree with you. Other businessmen don't give loans to just anybody. The Kabulis will, before you've blinked your eye—at a four-to-one return—and if you don't pay up, they make life very unpleasant."

Mr. Sharma—"You're right, Rupa. Who else would give? Well, let my brother grovel. I'd like to see who'll come from his father-in-law's to pay the money back."

Rupamati—"Where is his father-in-law going to get money to rescue him? I heard he got into a quarrel over a bad investment and lost everything."

Mr. Sharma—"When will ill-gotten wealth ever be secure? For one thing, his father got the inheritance of some man without a son in Burma he hardly knew. No way were they his real father- and mother-in-law! And then he himself has made his tenants feel the pinch, so they say. He went on increasing interest to anywhere from twenty-five to thirty percent and then seized their land. Even what you come by honestly isn't secure. Lakshmi is a fickle goddess. How can money earned from hundreds of people's tears be?"

Rupamati—"Can you just stand by and watch your own brother in his distress."

Mr. Sharma—"What can we do but watch? If we go on paying his loans he won't stop taking new ones. You've seen his ways and heard the mess he's in."

Rupamati—"But maybe he's wiser now. Before, his wife supplied whatever money he asked for, so he enjoyed things. But now that there's nowhere for money to come from, isn't he perhaps reforming?"

Mr. Sharma—"No, I don't think so. Even if you keep a dog's tail in a pipe for twelve years, it will come out more curled than ever. It will never be straight."

Rupamati—"Leave that to the future. Now the man from Kabul has robbed him of his respect. And in this cold season too. What a hard time he must be giving him! How much did he owe?"

Mr. Sharma—"It was 139 rupees and 24 annas."

Rupamati—"That has to be paid."

She insisted. She called Bagvir, gave him the money and sent him off.

Bagvir did everything of a practical nature in Mr. Sharma's house. After delivering the money, he returned. "That Kabuli was giving him one hell of a time! He kept him packed on the dark ground floor and was cursing him from outside. Once I was there, he brought him out. As soon as he saw me he turned red. Didn't say a thing." He narrated the whole episode.

Ravilal reached home, went directly upstairs and kicked his wife nearly to death. Had his daughters not cried aloud, she perhaps would have expired then and there.

Now it had become impossible for her to stay on. The next day she looked for a porter and went with her daughters back to her childhood home. The day after that, when Ravilal returned to eat, he found the main door locked. When he asked his neighbours, they told him that his wife had gone home.

ಐಞ

Chapter 20

Baral's daughter reached home at a trudger's pace. As the hills of Chepetar came into view, her heart stood still. Remembering her mother, she began to cry. Her mother always used to send porters to fetch her, and how happy she was when they returned together! How the villagers showed respect! They used to say that if they could please the daughter they would receive treats from the mother. All the women of her home had been kept under close control. Lakshmi, the goddess of wealth, had also been in residence. Who hadn't heard of the Barals from Besi? Now those ears heard of nothing but collapse and ruin. The local Jaisis[110] knew a hundred ways to trip people up and create misunderstandings; they were behind things, it was said. After the death of her mother, the treasury must have been inspected. She wondered what her father thought when he found so much money and jewellery missing. How could she show her face now?

Baral's daughter's erring mind cast up doubts. She even pondered turning around. That house again danced in front of her eyes. How could she go back to it? Her husband's behaviour hadn't changed. There wasn't a day she wasn't kicked. Bruises covered her body. What was there to eat? Even though she had spent money frugally, it was now all gone. Oh Lord, what shabby luckless karma she had! There were four daughters; how to look after them? The world appeared bleak to her.

By then she had reached home. Upon seeing the house, she began to weep, but when she looked at her daughters, who were also on the point of weeping, she brought herself under control. The house was desolate. They all entered in a hush. Only the youngest sister-in-law was there, sitting in a corner; her face, too, was

---

[110] A caste consisting of the offspring of a Brahmin man and Brahmin widow.

gloomy. Baral's daughter stood still. She ventured no further. What was this? Why such quietude today? If she asked, what words would her sister-in-law utter? But now when their eyes met, there was no way not to speak. But, good Lord, what to say? The things she was being forced to witness that day! Just last year people had come to the Daraundi bridge to welcome her. How the children had bubbled over! And what manners her sisters-in-law, too, had shown! Why today did she see no one? Why did no one speak? Why was her youngest sister-in-law wearing the face of one who had fled straight from a graveyard?

She was now finally home, and her feet had come to a halt. Wondering what the future held, she had the porter set his dosser down. Her daughters also sat down. She herself went up to her sister-in-law and began a conversation. "What's wrong? Aren't you well? You're not speaking. I don't see anyone home."

Her question drew a quick reply. "Wasn't it enough to ruin the whole house? What have you got in store for us now with your visit? What's left to do? You may be thinking that money will fall into your hands, but I wouldn't count on it. Your father left the country from the shock of losing his wealth; no one knows where he is. One of your brothers went to Gorkha, and another to Pokhara, to attend court cases. Their wives went home with their children. I'm here; my husband, our boy, your two little vixens. For six months we've been looking for someone to send them with to the city but didn't find anyone. We're in a fix. Now that you've come, you take them away. You can go either tomorrow or the day after."

These words worked like poison on Baral's daughter's heart. How her limbs must have stiffened in the same house she had once ruled over! It was no small matter for her to find herself on her back.

After a while her daughters arrived. They were unrecognizable—as if they would fall over with a puff. Their eyes were like nostrils, their faces lacked complexion, their cheeks were hollow, and their voices were nasal. Their attire was threadbare: blouses mended in seven or eight places, and dirty, torn homespun cloth wrapped over their head and shoulders. When she saw them, her heart was riven, her vision blurred, and her breath quickened. What to say? What to say? She hugged her daughters and cried out, "Oh Lord, that these eyes have to see such misfortune!" She lapsed into sobs.

Her sister-in-law was busy arranging things in the kitchen. Hearing the crying, she came and said, "Is this a good sign for a daughter to come and cry in the evening? You're still not satisfied to see what this house has come to? Who do you plan to swallow up with your omens? Wasn't the property enough?"

Baral's daughter remained silent. She had not the strength to reply. What could she have replied even if she had had the means to speak? There was none she had not hurt. Everyone had come to know that she had made off with the property underhandedly. The present rundown condition of the house was the result. She was regarded as the culprit. She remembered intermittently her other house. Her heart trembled. It frightened her to recall her husband's behaviour.

Madhuvan's youngest son, Pandit Trilochan Baral, came panting home. He was a large, big-bellied man. His earlier days, when his father and brother were managing the work, he had spent in bliss. He had indulged in entertainment. Now there was no getting around quarrels with the Jaisis and going to court. With his father no longer around, all responsibility fell upon him. He had to look after everything himself. The poor man was at his last gasp attending to the field work. Upon arriving home, he saw his sister, bowed to her and asked how she had been. "Where are you coming from? You didn't write about coming. How is your husband?"

This last query was pushing the limits. Why call down contempt upon herself by admitting the true state of affairs in her household? There was now no one to exclaim a sympathetic Good gracious! But why give them a free opportunity to say, You deserve it. She replied, "Everything is fine." With this evasion she tried to paste over things, but everyone knew about her husband's exploits.

It would be difficult for her to stay more than four or five days. The women waxed sarcastic to the point of unbearableness. They kept asking, "When are you going to the city? How long is the walk?" When she went to take meals, they gave her nothing but unseasoned and boiled dishes; those, too, plumped down in front of her. When she had cleared her plate of vegetables and curries, there was no second helping. At every level they were sending signals for her to clear out. They arranged for porters and put everything in shape.

Baral's daughter departed with her four daughters for Kathmandu. She reached Balaju but didn't have energy to go further. All sorts of thoughts played around in her head. She decided to spend a week in Balaju, at her best friend's house, thinking it not wise to go back home without finding out what was going on there.

Just four or five days after Baral's daughter had left her house Tunche came to raid it. Ravilal being unable to pay back the money on time, what other recourse did he have? Ravilal sold some of the remaining utensils and bedding, and some were taken away by shopkeepers. Poverty had now set in. Nothing was left to Ravilal except the clothes on his back. All this news reached Baral's daughter in Balaju. Here her husband was also living hand to mouth. Friends he used to fête and entertain pretended not to notice him even in open daylight. No one gave him the time of day. It was then that Ravilal came down with typhoid. He swooned and fell into a stupour, and began to talk gibberish. One old woman had a tender spot for him and gave him shelter. Thus he stayed in a rest-house. The poor woman did her best to tend to him, but she could not afford medicine.

Dahalni Bajyai went down to the Bagmati. She was a friend of the old woman. She learned about Ravilal and sent news to his mother. Rupamati became very upset upon hearing it. She herself went to the Bagmati. Her brother-in-law's condition caused her great worry. Physicians advised her to keep him where he was until he had made it or succumbed. Rupamati forgot all household work and put heart and soul into caring for him. After three days Ravilal was able to speak. He was carried home carefully on a carpet. Rupamati attended him on her own. She had read a book titled *Care, Love and Service to the Sick*. She nursed mindful of all its points, and soon her brother-in-law was well.

When Ravilal had gained some of his senses, he could feel someone putting a handkerchief moistened with eau de cologne on his forehead. Fluttering his eyes, he had the vague impression that it was Rupamati. Gradually he came fully to and was surprised to see the continuous labours and tender care his sister-in-law was expending on him. Oh, what an active spirit! At last he came to know his sister-in-law for who she was. His heart filled with gratitude. He felt uplifted. The work of love left a grand imprint on his heart. The veil of ignorance that had covered over his powers of thought was torn. The demoniacal impulses that resided in him and prevented bright thoughts from arising now disappeared at compassionate love's powerful spell, just as ghosts do by incantation.

He saw that his sister-in-law did love him. Everyone, in fact, had forgotten all his thousands of misdeeds and were now showing affection. The same flood of pure love—true and selfless—upon which this world stands had today welled up and made their hearts vessels of love. How would he repay the debt to his sister-in-law of having saved him from the jaws of death?

Now he would never say no to her. He would agree to anything she said, no matter what she asked him to do. He had now fully recovered from his illness. When he went out he did not care to see the Tharus Jhilke and Dhanamane. His appearance and behaviour had changed. He showed great respect to his brother- and sister-in-law, and to his mother. All were amazed to see such a great change come into his life. They were astounded that such an impertinent and misguided fellow was now in the state he was.

News arrived that Ravilal's wife was staying at her friend's home in Balaju. She had been through the mill. Rupamati had always wished that none of her family should suffer. She sent Bagvir accompanied by a woman to bring her back home.

How could Baral's daughter set foot in that house? By calling her back with news of her husband's illness were they trying to put her to shame? A host of doubts arose in her erring mind. Bagvir tried his best to explain, but she refused to go. He came back without her. But he had seen with his own eyes the dreadful condition Ravilal's wife was in. He described everything.

Rupamati was greatly shaken. The woes of her sister-in-law and nieces made her restless. The next day she herself went with Bagvir and a servant. She convinced her sister-in-law and nieces to come back home. It was easy to imagine how they had suffered, from their faces and what they wore. She got them all to change their old clothes for something new. She arranged a bedroom with beds and mosquito nets and all the other necessities. Her sister-in-law's arrogance was broken. Her false pride crumbled at what even in her wildest dreams she could not imagine—loving treatment from Rupamati.

Within two weeks Rupamati arranged for the marriage of the eldest daughter, and also started to look for a bridegroom for the second one. She made no distinctions when it came to food and dress. It was all too much. One day Ravilal's wife could no longer control herself. She dropped to Rupamati's feet and began to cry. Rupamati raised her immediately and said, "What are you doing?" She advised her instead to bow down at her mother-in-law's feet and make amends for past ill deeds done to her. The mother-in-law for her part forgot the distress she had undergone when she saw her daughter-in-law's remorse.

Ravilal still had not set eyes on his wife, his thoughts darkened at how she had taken him away from a heavenly house, from his brother, and from the mother who gave him birth. These sentiments, too, Rupamati set about erasing from of his mind little by little.

Mr. Sharma was very content with this new-found harmony among all members of the family. He would have to get his brother going again, and feeling that he had now learned his lesson and would not go astray, he contemplated sending him to the plains to do farming. The Luintels had transferred all their land in the Terai to

Rupamati. They had assembled large plots there by investing whatever they had. Rupamati's parents had enough to live on from their fields in the Kathmandu Valley, so the Terai land was put under Mr. Sharma. Rupamati thought of transferring this land to her sister-in-law. Mr. Sharma did not agree. She told him, "By the grace of God we have enough to live on, so all we need do is draw up the papers so that the land cannot be sold."

Ravilal for his part was happy to go to the plains. The prospect of work made him particularly so. After working two or three years, he acquired a taste for the place. He took his wife to live in Kataharban on the Bagmati. Three of his daughters had already married; the remaining one went along south. Now that he was working hard, there was no living from hand to mouth. He could have made lots of money if prices had been high, but even with present prices he had no problem surviving.

Mr. Sharma also saw his fortunes rise day by day. His income increased steadily. Rupamati had nothing to worry about. Her son was a boy of uncommon intelligence, who put his heart and soul into his studies. His grandmother was overjoyed.

ೞಓ

Chapter 21

Today there was a big gathering of women at Chattu's place. Rasbihari was talking very heatedly. Mr. Nepal's family was up for comment.

Rasbihari—"Did you see? Is it right or not to say people taste for themselves in this life the fruits of their good and evil? How your *subba*'s mother has had to praise the daughter-in-law she used to nag and tear into for nothing."

Chattu's wife—"Right. To break in her older daughter-in-law she pampered her younger one, and then *she* turned around and kicked *her*, and how!"

Chattu's younger sister—"The sin of making someone better than you cry and suffer will backfire immediately. Who's been through what she did when she split off from the rest with her husband? What entertainment!"

Chitravir Thapa's wife—"Ravilal himself had fruits to reap for making his mother cry. He had one foot in the grave. That he survived was luck."

Rasbihari—"Rupamati is really a brave lady. First she put up with her mother-in-law's rebukes. Later when her sister-in-law caused her so much trouble, she didn't utter one nasty word. On several occasions she got her brother-in-law out of fixes. At the end, when he was just about gone, she brought him back, cared for him and restored him to life. Bravo! That's how women should be!"

Chattu's wife and the other women had never been able to stand others being praised. But now they were all swayed by Rasbihari's discourse. All echoed his thoughts.

Rasbihari—"Once women go bad, they can really stick it to you. Look at Ravilal's wife—jealous something fierce! She said unspeakable things to her mother-in-law, and paid the consequences. The daughter-in-law who calls her mother-in-law bad is bad herself. She won't be able to run the house. It'll go to pot—no doubt about it. If a mother-in-law is bad she'll pay for her sins herself. Did Rupamati's mother-in-law suffer for all the wrong she did her or not? Did Rupamati make her suffer? And another thing: a wife who tries to win her husband over to her side by supplying him with heaps of money doesn't realize that she's spoiling him. Afterwards, once he's reduced her to poverty, that same husband will leave her; kick her out. By secretly lavishing wealth on her husband she spoils him and ruins her own home. You saw how Ravilal's wife wreaked total destruction. How the Lord did break her pride! At last she had to go and take refuge with Rupamati, and bow down to her mother-in-law."

Chattu's wife—"What are you saying? That her parents' home came to ruin that way?"

Rasbihari—"How can it come to any good when a daughter filches and creates havoc? And then you have Shushupal Baral bringing someone else's inheritance from Burma. He goes and lives in an old man's house, suddenly the old man dies, and the next day he makes off with all his property. He didn't even perform the death rituals. If wealth earned honestly, by sweating blood, doesn't last, how will it if gained by those means?"

Chattu's wife—"It wasn't only his wife who ruined Ravilal, it was his mother also."

Rasbihari—"You're right. Mothers spoil children by coddling rather than scolding them when they hear they've taken up bad habits. If they don't get the chance to fling around money after becoming teenagers, they won't go wrong so quickly. I'm not saying parents don't spoil children that way, but in this case isn't it possible Ravilal turned out the way he did because—even more than his mother—his wife provided him wads of money?"

Chitravir's wife—"But let me tell you, Luintelni Bajyai is really a wonderful woman, an incarnation of Lakshmi."

Rasbihari—"That's why her daughter also became a Lakshmi. Daughters turn out the way they're trained by their mothers. Luintelni Bajyai taught Rupamati housework well, so she's earned a good name. Baralni

Bajyai raised her daughter on a pedestal, and how has she fared?"

Chattu's wife—"Mr. Sharma is also big-hearted—bringing his wayward brother back home and setting him up."

Rasbihari—"You're right about that. How would she have brought her brother-in-law back without her husband's consent? But it was Rupamati who got them settled. Such women are one in a thousand—no, one in a million. If all women today were like her, this world of woes would turn into a sea of happiness. Now tell me, do you think other women would be willing to go through the constant suffering? If they followed Rupamati's guide, they'd be well on their way to hearing, 'Well done.'"

ಙಚ

PBH

OTHER TITLES FROM OUR DISTRIBUTORS PILGRIMS BOOK HOUSE

KATHMANDU, TREKS AND HIPPIES TOO
*By **Dorothy Mierow***
Based on her own experiences, Dorothy Mierow's absorbing and dramatic novel chronicles the adventures of Cindy Adams, a bright but confused college graduate who in the 1960s was among the first American Peace Corps Volunteers to be sent to Nepal, a small and remote Himalayan kingdom which, up to then, was isolated from the rest of the world. Aside from the Peace Corps, Nepal was also becoming the new found "Shangri-La" destination for the Asia-overland, vagabond hippie set. In those heady days, hash was legal, love was cheap and life was high. Struggling to make sense of an alien but exotic culture which she helps to bring from the middle ages into the 20th century. Cindy questions her own values and finds her way towards a fulfilling purpose of life.

175 pages Paperback ISBN 81-7303-049-5
Price: **US $ 5.50** Shipping: Sea/Air $1.50/$7.00

FAULTY GLASSES
*By **B.P. Koirala***
*Translated by **Keshar Lall***
In Faulty Glasses, Nepal's pre-eminent statesman, B.P.Koirala, re-creates a world of emotion in all its varied manifestations; love, loathing, compassion, jealousy, fear, affection, anger and pity.
Written in the late 1940s, his short stories of human interaction take place in the geographical locations throughout Nepal. They provide valuable insights into the everyday lives of the Nepalese people.

69 pages Paperback ISBN 81-7303-055-3
Price: **US $ 3.00** Shipping: Sea/Air $1.00/$3.00

THIRTY YEARS IN POKHARA
*By **Dorothy Mierow***
Nepal casts a spell on those who come to visit for a while and they stay longer and return again and again.

With Machhapuchare and the Annapurna Range as a background and subtropical flowering trees and picturesque lakes and scenes, Pokhara Valley is one of the most beautiful places in the world. It also has a diverse population and is rapidly modernizing its facilities to be worthy of being the most popular vacation destination in Nepal.

This is the story of its period of greatest development and change by an American Peace Corps Volunteer who came in the early 60s and stayed to develop a Natural History Museum and assist in the Annapurna Conservation Area Project. Thirty years of life in Nepal by an American who fell in love with Pokhara.

126 pages Paperback ISBN 81-7303-075-8
Price: **US $ 15.86** Shipping: Sea/Air $1.14/$7.32

CONFESSION
By Kavita Ram Shrestha
Translated by Larry Hartsell
Boldly written and controversial, this powerful translation is available for the first time in the English language. The Nepali characters of a sick woman, a dwarf and a whore portray frusted people which society creates but then turns into objects of hatred. Although it is a story of opposition to society's values, it is, as the author says, "a story that exists in all places, times and personalities." Introduction by Krishnachandra Singh.

75 pages Paperback ISBN 81-7303-033-2
Price: **US $ 4.00** Shipping: Sea/Air $1.00/$3.00

KHAIRINI GHAT
by Shankar Koirala
Translated by Larry Hartsell
After having lost himself for ten years in Calcutta, a weary traveller returns to his native village in the hills of Nepal to cope with political and social changes. Attempting to regain his former status, he resists the temptations of village women and manages the affairs of village life. It is an evocative narrative, which provides a rare glimpse of rural Nepal in the recent past that is slowly disappearing. "This small sensuous novel...packed with action...has all the ingredients of a best seller" - The Rising Nepal.

101 pages Paperback ISBN 81-7303-041-1
Price: **US $4.50** Shipping: Sea/Air $1.00/$3.00

GUESTS IN THIS COUNTRY: A DEVELOPMENT FANTASY
by Greta Rana

Becky Sidebottom, a recent university graduate, lands her first job as a Junior Programme Officer for an international aid agency in the third world state of Lapalistan. An innocent abroad, Becky quickly learns the ropes and gets caught up in a maelstrom of espionage, counter revolution, romance, pregnancy and tennis matches. This humorous but thought-provoking novel is a biting spoof about the new colonialism of development aid which benefits administrators and local elites more than the poor.

365 pages Paperback ISBN 81-7303-034-0
Price: **US $7.50** Shipping: Sea/Air $2.00/$9.00

These and other fine titles may be ordered directly. Credit card orders accepted by fax with card number, expiration date and signature. Request our free publication catalogue.

PILGRIMS BOOK HOUSE

P.O. Box 3872, Kathmandu, Nepal
Fax: [977-1] 424943. E-mail: info@pilgrims.wlink.com.np